"Challenger Bhodi Li, prepare to do battle."

Bhodi broke into a trot in the direction of the nearest outcrop. A red flicker played across his facemask and slashed diagonally across his shoulder. He nearly screamed in shock and pain. It was as though his skin were being seared in a bath of liquid fire.

Scrambling into the protective shadow of a rock wall, he caught a glimpse of a wide-hipped thick-legged figure in tan fatigues. Not human. Then rock chips showered down on Bhodi as a phaser bolt struck inches above his head, and he ducked out of sight.

Everything he had done so far had been defensive, he realized. *They act, I react. But that's not the way I fight. And if I keep it up, they're going to hunt me down for sure . . .*

PHOTON®

THE ULTIMATE GAME ON PLANET EARTH™

THIEVES OF LIGHT

MICHAEL HUDSON

BERKLEY BOOKS, NEW YORK

Photon and Photon logo are registered trademarks
of Photon Marketing, Ltd.
THE ULTIMATE GAME ON PLANET EARTH
is a trademark of Photon Marketing, Ltd.

THIEVES OF LIGHT

A Berkley Book/published by arrangement with
Photon Marketing, Ltd., DIC.

PRINTING HISTORY
Berkley edition/April 1987

ISBN: 0-425-09810-9

A BERKLEY BOOK® TM 757,375
Berkley Books are published by The Berkley Publishing Group,
200 Madison Avenue, New York, NY 10016.
The name ''BERKLEY'' and the stylized ''B'' with design are trademarks
belonging to the Berkley Publishing Corporation.

PRINTED IN THE UNITED STATES OF AMERICA

Author's Note

As is the case with nearly all heroes, there are many versions of Christopher Jarvis's story. Some, like the authorized biography released by the Chief Historian of the Photon Alliance, are colored by politics and security considerations. Others, like the popular fictions of Tyrrane Beldak, are a confusing blend of true and imaginary events. The various profiles assembled by journalists on free-press worlds are invariably incomplete even when they are accurate.

The following account represents the first attempt to combine the authority of official records, the honesty of independent journalism, and the emotional power of fiction in a single narrative. It is based on hundreds of hours of interviews with many of the principals in the story, including two rare interviews with Jarvis himself and thousands of official Photon documents and records, many previously unreleased. The portrait of events for which no witnesses or records could be located is based on a detailed psychogram of Christopher Jarvis prepared by Dr. J. T. Jarvis (no relation) of the Hillena Institute.

In short, what you are about to read is the truth dressed up as fiction. Christopher Jarvis the hero is here, but so is Christopher Jarvis the boy and man. I hope that you will come to know and admire them both, as I have.

—MICHAEL HUDSON
Terrake Station, 1987

PROLOG

Deep within a great space station orbiting a tiny blue-white star, a warrior labored at a task warriors despised. Perched on a special stool that safely supported his massive bulk yet let his thick, leathery tail swing freely, he sat at his work station and stared at a display screen.

The brownish-green skin of his forehead, almost invisible above a protruding snout that would have been at home on a Komodo dragon, was furrowed with frustration. His jaws parted, revealing a dozen smaller teeth to go with the six upper canines that showed even when his mouth was closed. He lashed the air with his tongue.

"Eheheh," the warrior growled. "There's never any end of combat reports." Then he resumed punching at the data entry keys with thick fingers.

His name was Nar-lex-ko-li-hon, which meant To-cowards-their-due in the language of his people. His people called themselves the Qeth—the Chosen—and their world Bree-nech—Peaceful Morning.

As first in a litter of six, Nar-lex-ko-li-hon had the right to carry his father's name, Fo-bek-tin—Glories-of-night. A poet's name, appropriate to the poet's spirit Nar-lex-ko-li-hon had inherited.

1

But the world into which he was born eighty-two cycles ago was gripped by a savage internecine war, and his destiny from birth had been to train as a soldier of the West and take up arms against the armies of the East. The times, rather than tradition, had dictated his naming.

It was the most pointless and brutal of wars, Qeth against Qeth, foot soldier against foot soldier, eventually costing both sides far more than complete surrender possibly could have. In the course of twenty-six cycles of fighting, the better part of two generations of nestlings were slain on the battlefield. The territorial boundary moved eight hundred miles east, twelve hundred miles west, and ended up a hundred miles from where it had been when war began.

At last a third generation rebelled against the ongoing slaughter and forced peace on the ruling classes of East and West alike. None was more glad than Nar-lex-ko-li-hon when the armistice came, for none had seen more clearly or closely the terrible price of the war.

On Union Day, as unfertilized eggs were exchanged between the First Breeders of the East and the West— symbolic hostages to guarantee the peace—he vowed never to fight again. From that day on, he considered his name an anachronism, and chose to be called only Li-hon—meaning Destiny.

But now, many years removed from that vow and a long way from Qeth, Li-hon was caught up in a much more far-reaching war. This time, he was not fighting over Qeth, but for it. This time, the enemy was not beings like himself, but demons out of a nestling's nightmare. This time, peace was not an option. This time, the only choices were death or victory.

The work station chirruped at Li-hon, and the display he had been working on faded away to black. "What is it?" he demanded of the communicator.

He was answered by the dulcet voice of the space station's central machine intelligence, formally known as the First Guardian. Though the computer itself was sexless, its voice and visualizations were unmistakably female, even maternal. "Recruitment alert, Nar-lex-ko-li-hon. A prospective candidate for the Guardians has been identified by the Monitor at Center 8053."

Li-hon craned his head ceilingward, flexing the cramped muscles of his massive neck. "That's on Earth," he said without much enthusiasm. "What's the candidate's name?"

"Christopher Jarvis. Within the Center he uses an alternate identity, Bhodi Li. The meaning of the alternate identity is unknown."

"Bo-di-li," Li-hon repeated. "In Qeth it would mean Battle-child."

"It is a meaningless coincidence," she rebuked him. "The individual in question is a young adult human—"

"Let me see the monitor tapes," Li-hon interrupted.

The screen brightened. As though he were a spider on the ceiling, Li-hon looked down into a large arena where a dozen helmeted figures skulked behind the cover of barricades, raced up ramps, and hid in tunnels, clutching infrared pistols in their hands.

"That one," the First Guardian said as a bright red spotting circle enclosed one of the players.

Li-hon did not need help identifying Jarvis. In the brief time he had been watching, the Terran had scored against three of his opponents with what seemed impulsive and ill-considered charges. He was now poised to make a thrust toward the base goal, located in an alcove near the top of a ramp. Two of Jarvis's opponents lurked in hiding near the goal, ready to defend it.

"There is a certain recklessness to this one," the First Guardian observed.

"There is also an intensity not often found in humans,"

Li-hon said. "What projection do you make for his success?"

"The value approaches one that he will achieve the threshold score very shortly," she said. "The probability he could meet our requirements and become a Guardian of the Light is considerably less, perhaps no more than point-three-eight."

"He interests me."

"He is yours for claiming, though I would recommend against it. The species is ill-suited to the challenges of this war. Parcival is an exception."

"I claim him nonetheless. Is Parcival on station?"

"He is."

"Then will you have a scoutship readied for us?"

"As you wish," the First Guardian said disapprovingly. "Even though I suspect you of feigning interest in Jarvis in order to avoid timely completion of your logwork."

It's not out of the question, Li-hon thought. But this time at least, I have other reasons.

"My interest is real," he said, rising from the stool to his full seven-foot height. "This one I want to see myself."

CHAPTER 1

The doodle in the margin of Christopher Jarvis's notepad was quickly growing to epic proportions.

It had started out as a caricature of the President, then mutated into a creature that would have done a special-effects magician proud. Finally it dissolved into a mass of whorls and curlicues that climbed up the side margin and spilled out like an ink tsunami onto the white space at the top of the page.

The whole business had occupied him for the better part of ten minutes. By any standard, it was a success. That was ten minutes less he had to listen to Mrs. Martini drone on about the phylum Bryophyta, ten minutes closer to the end of the period and Friday's final bell.

"Christopher—"

It took Jarvis several heartbeats to realize that he had been caught. His pen stopped moving. His greenish-blue eyes flicked upward from the paper. At last he raised his head and looked toward the front of the classroom. The look on Mrs. Martini's face said that she'd been waiting for some time for him to respond. An amused titter, female-variety, confirmed it.

Though his gaze never wandered from Mrs. Martini's

face, Jarvis knew the titter came from Denise Barrows, two rows to the right and one seat forward. It was not just that he knew her voice. He was aware of everything she did and everything about her—the way her long black hair fell across one eye as she worked at her desk, the way she carried her books on one hip as she moved past him in the corridor, the half smile that always preceded her easy laugh.

Jarvis liked her laugh—except when it was at his expense. Which it stood a good chance of being before Mrs. Martini was done with him.

"Yes, Mrs. Martini?" he said with studied innocence.

"I *had* asked you a question."

"I know," he said. "I didn't understand it."

Raising an eyebrow questioningly, the petite biology teacher repeated, "I had asked you to explain what hornworts are?"

Conscious of Denise, Jarvis did not want to admit he didn't know. But there were other options.

"Hornworts?" Jarvis said lightly. "I think that's something you get from handling tuba players."

Laughter filled the room, uniting the class with him and against Mrs. Martini. But it was a costly escape, for his teacher's face frosted over.

"See me after class," she said, and turned to a student in the front row for the answer.

Denise glanced his way, hair falling over one eye, and laughed amusedly.

At him.

Slumping back in his seat, Jarvis tried to look like he was listening. But his mind was begging, *Get me out of here—*

When the bell finally rang, Jarvis waited until most of the other students had noisily filed out before gathering himself together and approaching Mrs. Martini. She ignored him as she collected her teaching notes and placed them in a soft-sided briefcase.

"I have to catch the bus," he said finally, prodding her into taking note of him.

"Since when do seniors ride the bus?" she asked without looking up. "Don't you ride with—David Reynolds, isn't it? He'll wait for you."

Not long, Jarvis thought. Not with a Friday four o'clock reservation at the Photon Center and a tournament tomorrow. "Not long."

"Then he's not much of a friend, is he?" Mrs. Martini asked, retreating behind her desk. "In any case, you only live about eight blocks from here. Staying a while won't be any hardship."

Jarvis crossed his arms over his chest in an unconscious defensive gesture. "You seem to know a lot about me."

For the first time she looked at him. "For better or for worse, Christopher, you're the kind of student that teachers are aware of."

"I guess you're going to tell me that this time it's for worse," Jarvis said. "Look, I'm sorry I made fun of you. I didn't mean anything personal by it."

"You didn't make fun of me," she said, sitting in her chair. "You had a chance for a cheap joke and you took it. Probably because the truth was a little too uncomfortable."

"The truth?"

"That you weren't listening. That you weren't prepared. How many chapters behind are you in your reading?"

"Just a couple."

"Just a couple," she repeated. "When are you planning to catch up?"

"I'll be ready for the test."

"Just ready enough to just barely get by," the woman said pointedly. "I don't understand you, Christopher, and I don't mind admitting it. I looked at your file, your aptitude scores. You can handle this material with ease. But you don't seem to care enough to make the effort for excellence. What's going on?''

Jarvis bristled. ''If you're trying to ask me if I'm having a problem with drugs, the answer is no.''

Shaking her head, Mrs. Martini answered, ''I'm trying to ask how I can help you get more out of your ability.''

Jarvis dropped his arms to his side and slipped his hands into the pockets of his jeans. ''Look, I only took Botany Survey because I needed a senior science course and it was the only one without a lab. That makes me no different than half the class.''

''And that's enough excuse for you? That there's others who don't care either?''

Christopher sighed. ''Mrs. Martini, I know you mean well and all that. It's just that I don't see any sense to memorizing things that I can dig out of a database in a thirty-second dialup with my dad's PC. There's a lot more facts out there than I've got brain cells.''

''Even if you're right, there's something to be said for learning to think.''

''I do all right in that department. Isn't that what those tests said?''

She stared at him. ''You think you have the world pretty well figured out, don't you?''

''The part of it I know, anyway.''

''It's such a shame. I'd love to see you go all-out sometimes,'' she said with a shake of her head.

He smiled and ran his fingers back through his blond hair. ''Come down to the Center sometime.''

''The what?''

''The Photon Center.'' He flexed his muscles and struck a combat pose, knees flexed, hand gripping an imaginary phaser pistol. ''Meet Bhodi Li, champion of justice.''

Her look was one of disdain. "It's a game, Christopher. It's not life."

"Not life," he corrected. "Life and death. Is there anything else you wanted to talk to me about, Mrs. Martini?"

She threw her hands in the air resignedly. "No."

David Reynolds was waiting for him at the curb outside the school's main entrance, the engine of his 1970 Skylark convertible rumbling impatiently, his slightly shaggy black hair blowing in the breeze.

"Almost gave up on you," Reynolds said, slipping back behind the wheel as Jarvis climbed in from the other side. "Figured she was using you as mulch for her hornworts."

"Nothing so serious."

The car lurched as Reynolds coaxed the shift lever into drive. "Which speech was it?"

"The worried-about-my-future speech," Jarvis said. "Didn't have much zip to it, though. It seemed like she felt like she ought to be pissed at me, but couldn't quite muster the energy."

"Well, it's Friday afternoon for her, too," Reynolds said, gunning the engine as he guided the car through the mostly empty parking lot.

"True," Jarvis said. "It's probably just as tiring to be boring as it is to be bored."

The lot outside the Photon Center was more than half full, which meant a crowd inside. Though they were in time for the first match of the hour, they were late enough that they ended up on opposing teams for the first time in months, Jarvis with the Red, Reynolds with the Green.

As he strapped on his chest pod, which bore the infrared sensor, and the battery belt which powered it, Jarvis sized up the opposition. All but one was familiar, and the new-comer was a nervous-looking thirteen-year-old who would almost certainly end the match with a negative score.

Beside David, who used the name Kuda Lambda, there were four other strong players on the Green team. Though he knew what to expect from them in the arena, he did not even know their real names. He knew only their Photon names—Gor, Black Eagle, Oz, and Mordred. Together with Kuda Lambda, they would provide a stronger than usual challenge.

So much the better, Jarvis thought, pulling the helmet down over his head and adjusting the visor. *There aren't any twinkies on a tournament team.*

Jarvis showed considerably less interest in the members of his own team. The six-and-a-half-minute matches were fast-paced enough that, in a pickup match like this, most of what passed for strategy developed spontaneously on the run. Besides, most of his success at the game had come as a loner.

That didn't mean that there was no benefit to having someone watching your back, but successful team play was more a product of practice than planning. Warriors that fought together often developed an almost instinctive synergy that made them more effective together than separately. But strangers who tried to duplicate that interaction usually ended up worse off than if they had all fought solo.

The warning alarm sounded, and the combatants filed in to take their places in the arena. While the referee ran through his familiar list of admonitions, Jarvis caught Reynolds's eye and nodded, as though offering a salute. Reynolds grinned back and touched his gloved finger to the side of his helmet.

"Welcome, Photon Warriors. Commence strategic ma-neuvers at audible command," boomed the canned voice of the Master Computer. "Signal: five . . . four . . . three . . . two . . . one . . ."

Colored lights began to flash and the pulsing beat of rock music filled the arena as the players dashed for their chosen objectives. Bhodi Li sprinted up a ramp toward the sniper's nest on the forward deck, then flung himself flat on his stomach as two Green players came storming up another ramp from the opposite direction.

Before his opponents had even seen him, Bhodi had tagged each of them with the beam from his pistol. *Twenty points off the top,* Bhodi thought, scrambling to the left for the shelter of a low wall.

Another Red team player charged up the ramp, intent on the still-empty sniper's nest. But before he could reach it, Mordred appeared at the mouth of a side tunnel and raised his phaser.

The sucker ambush—that's your style, Bhodi thought. As Mordred tried to zero in on the running Red, Bhodi Li raised up from behind the wall and zapped him. Then, before Mordred could even look up to see who had made the speakers in his helmet buzz angrily, before his intended victim could see to whom he owed thanks, Bhodi Li was gone, on the move again.

Already he was attuned to the flow of the match and moved through the arena almost without thinking. Prowling the tunnels and ramps, pouncing from unexpected vantages, he ran up his score as he ran through the ranks of the Green team. Oz, Gor, even Black Eagle joined Mordred among his victims.

But at no point did he pause to gloat or savor his success. In Bhodi Li's concept of the game, his real opponent was time, the real objective to run up the score being credited to his name by the microcomputers monitoring the game. It was why he fought almost exclusively as a loner, even to sacrificing teammates for a few more hits, a few more tens of points. His entire defense was his relentless offense.

For Bhodi had a mountain to climb: the arena record of 2500 points. The record had been set by his friend Evan Kyley, a rangy teen a year older than Bhodi. Bhodi had been there when it happened, waiting for his own match and watching from the visitors gallery high above the arena. It had been an astonishing performance. It had also been Kyley's last match; a week later he left on a cross-country backpacking trip, and Bhodi had not heard from him since.

In perhaps a hundred matches since, Bhodi had scored more than 2000 points just five times, all in the last six weeks. The record was in reach, and that knowledge made him drive himself even harder. Almost as though there were tumblers spinning inside his head, he knew a good run from an average one. They had a feel all their own, his gambles paying off, his anticipations proving true.

This was a good run. But there was no way to crack the record without at least one successful assault on the Red goal and the two hundred points that came with it. Busy preying on the Red warriors, he had neglected that objective far too long. The final minute of the match was slipping away.

But there might still be enough time, though not enough for stealth. More directly than was his habit, Bhodi closed on the far end of the arena: down a ramp, along a narrow corridor past the bunker, left through a tunnel, then a dash across an open area to hide in a foxhole just twenty feet from the goal.

There were three Greens protecting the goal, Oz among them. He would have to take out all three to have a chance to deliver the required three consecutive shots into the heart of the goal. There was no more cover. He would simply have to shoot faster and more accurately than his opponents.

But just as he was about to make his charge, the speakers in his helmet buzzed angrily in his ears, signifying that he himself had been hit. His phaser momentarily disabled by the hit, he crouched and turned quickly to see who had gotten him.

It was David, standing not ten feet away and wearing a self-satisfied smile. Touching the barrel of his phaser to his temple, David returned the salute Bhodi had given him at the start. Then he slipped away before Bhodi's phaser returned to life.

Irritated at having been thwarted, Bhodi took one step to pursue David, then stopped and looked up as the overhead lights went to full white and the endgame signal sounded.

Not today, Bhodi Li thought resignedly, pushing his visor up. *Not today—*

"Thanks a lot, pal," Bhodi said, falling in step beside David as they left the arena for the changing area. "That's the first time I've been zapped in three weeks."

"I know. Took a little extra pleasure in it for that."

"Where were you the whole time, anyway? I don't think I saw you the whole match."

"Stalking you," David said brightly. "I knew you almost never look back. I wanted to see if I could pick you off without you ever getting me."

"Well, you did, damn your eyes."

"I didn't think I was ever going to catch up to you," David confessed. "You spent an awful long time standing in the foxhole. A long time for you, that is."

"The best cover is the kind you don't depend on for long."

"It's a shame you forgot that there at the end," David jibed.

Inside the changing area, they stopped in front of the wide-screen television suspended from the ceiling on which the match and individual player's scores were displayed. The Red team had won a slight victory, with most of the points beside the name BHODI LI. The more balanced Green team had five warriors over six hundred. Beside the name KUDA LAMBDA was the number 110.

"That's pathetic," Jarvis said, elbowing his friend as they turned away from the screen. "A hundred and ten?"

"Hey, I already told you, I did what I set out to. I wouldn't have cared if it was minus ten, as long as I didn't lose the ten points at your hands."

"Gee, thanks. What a buddy."

"Take it as a compliment."

"I'm trying."

"Your problem is you're too single-minded. There's more to this game than racking up high scores."

"No, there isn't," Bhodi said, unbuckling his battery belt and surrendering it to the attendant. "And you'll be glad of my two thousand points tomorrow in the tournament."

"You won't get two thousand points tomorrow," Reynolds said pointedly. "Not against the Shrike's team."

"Sure I will," Jarvis said cheerfully. "You can do what you did today, only turn around and protect my back instead of shooting me in it."

"I don't know," Reynolds said, rubbing his chin in an exaggerated caricature of indecision. "You'd do the same for me, right?"

"Sure. As soon as you're as good as I am."

"Today I was better."

"Is that what this is all about? Bragging rights?"

"Damn straight. And I've got 'em."

"But who knows it, except me and you?" Jarvis gestured toward the scoring screen. "They look at that and see something else."

Reynolds grinned crookedly. "You'll never understand, but nobody else has to know. You and me is enough."

"You're right," Jarvis said soberly. "I don't understand." He jerked his head toward the door. "Come on. Denise will be at the drive-in by now. Let's swing by for a shake."

"She's a lost cause," Reynolds warned, idly spinning the car keys on his forefinger.

Jarvis shook his head. "There's no such thing."

CHAPTER 2

Martin's Drive-In made a serviceable archetype for that species of home-grown fast-food restaurant that seems to exist in the shadow of every high school. Hand-lettered signs promoting permanent Specials shared the windows of the tiny square building with generic photographs of burger platters and pizza slices. The unpaved parking lot that surrounded it made a perfect showcase for new Firebirds and old but lovingly maintained Darts and Malibus alike.

Inside Martin's, freezers, fryers and grills crowded a kitchen no larger than a summer porch, and teenaged girls in tan smocks and paper caps ferried shake cups and plastic baskets of fries through the narrow aisles to the order window. The most popular item on the menu was the half-pound Raider Burger, which was named after the school's athletic teams and in most years was considerably more imposing.

It was nearly five when Reynolds and Jarvis reached the drive-in. The after-school drop-ins were thinning out, and the early-evening cruisers had yet to gather. Even so, a dozen vehicles were scattered around the lot, the same music blasting from high-power radios in three of them.

Reynolds slid his Skylark neatly between a black-glassed

van and Denise Barrows's rusting Volkswagen Beetle, and he and Jarvis vaulted out.

"Hey, Chris," someone called as they were spotted. "Martini give you a hard time?"

Jarvis grinned in the direction the voice had come from and raised a hand in greeting. "Nah," he called back. "No blood."

"Probably just wanted to show you her hornwarts," another voice chipped in.

Swiveling his head, Jarvis saw that it was Kid Vandergriff. A junior who looked like a freshman (thus his nickname) but circled like a hopeful puppy around the seniors, Vandergriff hadn't been in the biology lab for the confrontation.

Brightening appreciatively at the discovery his joke had not only been remembered but been repeated, Jarvis took note of the underclassman's marching-band jacket and shot back, "Which she caught from you, the way she told it. When are you going to see a doctor?"

Jarvis and Reynolds continued across the lot toward the order windows, calling greetings to others they knew. As they neared the building, Jarvis scanned through the odd bare patch of glass for Denise.

"Do you see her?"

"In the back. I think she's working the food window."

Without a word but both knowing why, they drew up short and stood talking about the tournament, until Denise returned to the counter with the order for the young family waiting there.

"Hey, Denise," Jarvis said, stepping forward. He rested his folded arms on the counter, which brought his face down to her eye level. "How's it going?"

"Fine, until you got here," she said cheerfully. "What do you want?"

"A big Pepsi—and a date."

"The Pepsi you can have," she said, turning away.

Reynolds whistled sympathetically and leaned back against the counter beside Jarvis. "I warned you."

"She just hasn't learned to appreciate my better qualities yet," he said with a shrug.

It was said as an aside, but Denise reappeared with Jarvis's drink in time to hear it. "You have no better qualities," she said crisply. "Ninety-three cents."

"You're so cold to me," he said, digging in his pocket for change.

"You're confusing me with the drink. Me, I just don't care. You know the feeling."

"What do you mean? Today in biology? What's the problem?"

Head cocked to the right and hands on her hips, she stared at him a moment, as if deciding whether to continue the conversation. "Your problem is that you're always performing for the audience," she said finally.

"I am not." His reflexive denial was sincere. *What is she talking about?* he wondered.

Denise shook her head resignedly. "I've got customers waiting," she said looking past him.

"But—"

"Get lost, Jarvis," she said pointedly.

Looking past Denise, Jarvis saw Fritz Martin, the owner, come out from behind the grill and start in their direction. Reluctantly, he turned away.

"I warned you," said Reynolds cheerfully.

"I'm just starting."

"You're out of your mind. All you're going to get from her is the back of her hand."

"She doesn't know me."

"Yeah, that's right. She probably thinks you're what you seem to be."

Jarvis missed the irony. "Well, sure. I mean, I don't

care if her family lives in a mobile home. But she doesn't know that."

"A twentieth-century Cinderella, and you the misbegotten prince."

This time the irony penetrated. "Make all the fun you like. I'm not giving up."

"Preps in love."

"I'm no Prep."

They had reached the car. "To her you are," Reynolds said, then hesitated. "If you're that determined—"

"I am. She's the one."

Reynolds sighed. "I'm probably going to regret telling you this, but she's going to be at the tournament tomorrow."

Jarvis perked up immediately. "To see me?"

"Dream on," he said, climbing behind the wheel. "No, Joanne's coming to watch her brother. Denise and a couple of the other girls are going with her."

"How do you know?"

Reynolds started the Skylark's engine. "Joanne told me. Anyway, even if she's not coming to see you—"

"I'll make sure she notices me."

"That's what I was afraid of." Reynolds looked back over his shoulder as he nudged the car into reverse. "Where to, rejected suitor?"

"Home."

Reynolds spun the steering wheel and then the wheels. "Prepville Express, all aboard."

Despite the fact that Jarvis did not feel it strongly himself, there was, in truth, a potent classism among the students at Montclair Senior High. Superficially, the cliques divided along their principal interests: academics, sports, or tomorrow-be-damned fun. But the underlying discriminator was money.

The classism was expressed daily by the names the

various cliques gave themselves, or had given to them. The Hall Rats were proud of their name; some even wore it embroidered on jeans or embossed on jackets. The Preps hated theirs, but were for the most part proud of the things that made them different—trendy clothes, new cars and ample pocket money.

Beyond the Preps, Jocks and Hall Rats there was also a silent, nearly invisible middle class within the school, without enough of an identity to even warrant a nickname. As many as two in five students belonged here, among them Denise—though because of her looks, she drew continuing attention from the Jocks and at times was taken for a Jockette.

Jarvis had friends in every clique. He was bright enough to not be in awe of the Preps, even if his grades didn't reflect it; like them, it was presumed that he would go to college. With his blond hair and tanned, trim body, he looked like an athlete and knew their language, though his last organized competition had been as a sophomore on the track team. And the occasional flash of wildness endeared him to the underclass, who thought of him as kin under the skin.

But to those looking for a quick or simple reading, where and how Jarvis lived placed him firmly among the Preps. Home was a five-bedroom split-level in a new subdivision north of town. The sprinklered lawn was always lush green. There were golf clubs in the garage, a deck with a barbecue in the backyard, and a ten-year-old sister with braces. Except for Jarvis's own room and the unfinished third of the basement, the house typically looked as though it were ready to be shown to prospective buyers.

His mother, Barbara, called it comfortable, and perhaps it was nothing more than that to her. But Jarvis had been in enough of his classmates' homes since they'd come to the community three years ago to know better, heard enough of them say, "Boy, this is *nice*" on their first visit.

Jarvis had trouble accepting such compliments gracefully. Part of the reason was that, after all, it wasn't his, was it? It was Barbara and Joshua's house, paid for with her tax consultancy fees and his office manager's salary. But the major reason was that Jarvis would have gladly traded it for something with a little texture, something containing a slightly less predictable and less ordered life.

Something less boring, if honesty compelled him to confess—

David dropped him off at the entrance to the cul-de-sac where his house sat, beeped a goodbye, and sped off. His hands empty except for the well-doodled, blue school folder that contained the American History assignment due Monday, Jarvis ambled along the sidewalk as though neither he nor anyone else cared when he arrived.

But someone did. Almost the moment he turned up the driveway, he was accosted by his sister Felicia. The ten-year-old dashed out through the front door, jumped off the side of the porch, and headed straight toward him across the grass.

"It's about time you got home," she scolded. "Where is it? Where's the kit?" Then she saw his nearly empty hands, stopped short, and ran back toward the house, this time crying plaintively, "Mom, he forgot it. Make him go back—"

The moment he had seen her, he remembered. Three days in a row he'd been asked to bring home the draftsman's kit, a dozen shiny little compasses and other drawing tools in a deep blue felt-lined case. He had taken it to school for some now-forgotten project, and it had been residing under the clutter at the bottom of his locker for more than two months.

He followed Felicia into the house just as his mother was coming down the stairs in response to her plaint. She was wearing a white slip, and her makeup seemed to be incomplete—obviously she and Dad were going to be going out, which meant dinner would be courtesy of Chef Swanson or Chez Del Monte tonight.

"Hello, Christopher. What's happening down here, Felicia?" she asked.

"Chris forgot the kit," she said with fierce childish indignation. "He promised and I need it this weekend. He's got to go back and get it."

"Oh, Chris," Barbara said with cow eyes of disappointment. "You didn't forget again—"

"I had to stay and talk to Mrs. Martini about biology, and Dave almost left without me. I didn't even have time to go to my locker."

In truth, he had gone to his locker, but on a dead run, pausing only enough to throw in his unneeded texts and notebook. His excuse was true in principle, at least, he consoled himself—it was the distraction of Mrs. Martini and the resultant haste that made him forget.

"What about going back?"

"It's too late."

"Aren't any of the teams practicing tonight? You should still be able to get in—"

"The hallways are blocked off with gates at four. I couldn't get to my locker." He turned to his sister. "I'm sorry, Felicia. I didn't mean to forget."

"Yes, you did," she fumed, then turned on her heel and fled up the stairs.

"This is too much, Chris," Barbara said, shaking her head. "You've really disappointed her. She was counting on working on her space station design this weekend. I thought you were going to write yourself a note?"

"I did," he confessed. "I left it on my dresser this morning."

"Oh, Chris," she said again. "Why were you in such a hurry? It wasn't that game, was it?"

"We were scheduled for a four o'clock match—"

"How much difference would two minutes more have made?"

"David was driving. I didn't have any choice—"

She clucked. "You're going to have to start being more considerate of your sister, not to mention more reliable. Isn't there any way that you can get the kit for her?"

"Sure. But I don't think you want me breaking into school."

Despite herself, his mother smiled. "That might not be the best idea," she agreed, her expression turning thoughtful. "Well, that is your father's kit, after all, and it is twenty years old. I guess I'll take your sister out shopping tonight, and we'll see if we can't find something that'll be all hers."

When he nodded and took a step toward the kitchen, she quickly added, "But Monday that kit comes home with you and goes back in the desk drawer where it belongs, even if I have to have you called out of your last class to remind you."

"I'll remember," he promised as he rounded the corner.

"And don't think this means that you're off the hook," she called after him, then turned and headed upstairs to complete her toilette.

But it did, in fact, mean he was off the hook, and that was nothing new. As a rule, his mother was unable to stop herself from rescuing him from the consequences of his own bollixations. Whether it was some sort of favoritism toward him (his sister's charge) or simply her desire to keep family peace (his father's opinion), he had profited from it more times than he could count.

That awareness had not yet led to any guilt, and this incident wasn't going to be the exception. He hadn't *meant* to forget, after all. And Felicia would be happier with her new tools—read toys—than if he had remembered the first time he'd been asked.

So it had all really worked out for the best, he told himself as he studied the back of the box his dinner had just emerged from. *Christopher Jarvis, catalyst for growth and progress*, he thought to himself. *Better living through amnesia. Now—five and a half minutes on high, then rotate a half turn—*

CHAPTER 3

For once, Christopher Jarvis awoke on a Saturday morning before his sister had a chance to invade his bedroom and wake him. There was none of his customary heavy-lidded groaning and stretching. His body was alive with energy and anticipation, as though it were ready for the tournament to begin that moment.

But the clock on his cluttered dresser advised him that it was just past 6:30, too early even to start helping with the family's traditional Saturday morning breakfast. The window of his bedroom faced east, and he sat on the sill in the T-shirt and briefs he'd slept in to watch the sun rise over the little copse of trees across the street.

As he sat, he thought a little about Mrs. Martini, a little about Denise. But most of the time he spent envisioning the arena he would enter at ten o'clock, cataloging its shadowed hiding places, visualizing his own success there.

In an idle moment in study hall, Jarvis had once paged through a copy of *Sports Illustrated* containing an article on the new breed of sports psychologists. Though he had skipped over the piece, he was nevertheless following the advice of one of the leading psychemasters profiled in it: Visualize the moment. See yourself in the act of hitting the clutch home run, breaking the tape in record time, sinking the winning free throw. Prepare your mind for the challenge, and your body will respond.

By seven, he was hearing the tell-tale sounds of other family members stirring and started to dress. It was one of the rules of Saturday breakfast that no one came to the table in nightclothes or robe. Mom insisted. It was her show, and had run three years without a missed performance. He remembered when she had instituted the now-entrenched ritual:

"We're all busy, every one of us, from Dad to Felicia, and that's good. But weekends have been just too crazy. Saturday morning is the only time in the whole weekend that I can be sure everyone will be here," she told the family. "So I'm going to see that we have at least one chance to talk to each other and one good meal in the weekend. This is how it's going to be—"

Standing at his dresser combing his thick, medium-short blond hair, Jarvis smelled coffee. By the time he reached the stairs, the irresistible smell of bacon frying had joined it. Downstairs, he found Felicia watching cartoons in the family room, and his mother in the kitchen. He joined her there and wordlessly started splitting English muffins with a fork.

"This is the big day," she said as she puttered at the stove. "Did I tell you that your father and I are going to come watch?"

More importantly, so is Denise. "It's not like the school gym," he warned. "The only place you can see the whole arena from is the rail of the observation deck. If you want a spot at it, you'll have to get there early."

"Well, what time are you planning to get there?"

"I have to leave right after breakfast. The team's meeting at the Center at nine, to go over things."

"Oh, that early? And when do you play?"

"Fight," Jarvis corrected. "In the first round, we're in the third match. Ten-thirty or so. After that, when we go back in depends on who beats who."

"I don't know, Chris," she said dubiously. "I have some things I promised to take over to Marjorie's this morning. I wasn't expecting to have to be there an hour and a half early to see you play."

Jarvis did not bother to correct her a second time. "You could probably see all right coming later." He hesitated, then added, "You guys really don't have to come at all if you're busy. I understand."

"No, no. We'll be there," she said, reaching out and patting his forearm. "I know it's important to you."

"It is. It's going to be a big day."

"And we'll be there to share it," she reassured him. "Tell you what. We'll leave right after breakfast and I'll drop you off on the way over to Marjorie's. Your Dad and Felicia can clean up the dishes, and I'll swing back for them later. We'll be there for your game."

Jarvis smiled. "Match, Mom."

"That's what I meant," she said, hands clutched together over her bosom girlishly. "Oh, the bacon. Where's my spatula?"

Despite good intentions, it was 9:15 before the Buick Century driven by Jarvis's mother coasted into the parking lot of the Photon Center. By then the asphalt was crowded with parked cars, players and their families on foot, and slowly moving cars whose drivers were jockeying for the remaining parking places.

"Just turn left here and let me out," Jarvis said, quickly sizing up the situation. "You don't want to get caught in that mess."

"What? Where?"

One hand on the door catch, he pointed out the windshield. "Just head for the exit," he said, opening the door and hopping out of the slowly moving vehicle. As his feet touched the pavement, he reached back in to snatch his gym bag off the seat, called, "See you later," then slammed the door shut.

As he turned toward the building, there was a whirring sound, and the passenger door window slid down."Christopher—good luck. I love you."

Jarvis turned back.

"Excuse me, good lady. You must have made an error," he said with mock dignity. "I am Bhodi Li, Photon Warrior." But before he dashed away, he bent down to peer inside the car and added, "But if I see this Christopher, I'll give him your message."

His mother smiled bemusedly. "Thank you—Bhodi."

Inside, Jarvis collected the other five members of his team from the couch they had commandeered in the lobby. He also collected from them some grief for being late.

"We were starting to think you weren't coming," David Reynolds said, standing as Jarvis approached. "Figured you'd be the first one here."

"My family slowed me up."

"Me, I figured maybe you hadn't gotten enough sleep during biology and were trying to catch up," piped Brian Duane from atop the back of the couch.

"Hey, that's my training program you're making fun of," Jarvis fired back with a grin. "Never stand when you can sit and never sit when you can lie down."

"I hope that's not your strategy for today," Greg Morse said worriedly. Morse was a wiry youth with jet-black hair and a premature collection of worry lines that he had come by honestly. "Can we talk about what we're going to do when we get in there?"

"We're going to win," Jarvis said pointedly. "Don't even think about any other possibility."

"I think Greg means he'd like to talk about strategy," Duane interjected.

"Strategy is very simple," Reynolds said drily. "Shoot them more often than they shoot us."

"Real funny, Dave," Morse said, his tone revealing his irritation.

"Jesus, another one with no sense of humus. Look, Greg, you tell me what good anything more complicated than that will be after thirty seconds in there."

Apparently trying to forestall the budding argument, Dennis Waverly spoke up for the first time. "I'll take the base goal. I don't mind."

"We ought to have two defenders," Morse said quickly.

"I'll stay back, too," offered Robert White, the sixth member of the team. White was also known as "Don't-Call-Me-Bob" White, for obvious reasons; he claimed that the three fender-benders he had had in his father's car were part of his long-delayed revenge on his parents.

"You can't just stand around there, though," Jarvis said warningly. "You've got to be active. If you wait for them to come to you, you're done."

"Should we go 2-2-2—two defenders, two snipers, two attackers?" asked Duane. "I'd like to go up front with Bhodi."

"I want David," Jarvis said, but the moment he got the words out Reynolds started shaking his head.

"I'll take the bunker and Greg can take the engine room," he said, ignoring Jarvis's hard looks. "If we're in this as long as we think we should be, everyone will get a turn everywhere."

Jarvis drew back wonderingly. "I hope you don't mean I ought to tend goal."

"I'd like to try it once," Reynolds said easily. "It'd

probably drive the other team nuts trying to figure out where the hell you were.''

''Well, we're sure as hell not going to try it today.''

''I thought you'd say that,'' Reynolds said, and turned to Waverly. ''I'm going to try to rotate back through the goal area off and on, and I think Greg ought to, too. I don't want them to be too sure of how we're deployed. If we can keep them wondering, we can slow them down.''

''Come on,'' Jarvis said, his annoyance with Reynolds translating into impatience. ''It's going to be crowded in the equipment room. We'd better get our gear. Some of us need to change, too—unless the Shrikes paid you to wear that white shirt during the match,'' he added, looking straight at Morse.

''Nope. It's coming off.''

''Not here, please!'' Reynolds said, leaping back and making a cross of his forefingers as though warding off a vampire. ''There's women and children present. Spare their innocent lives—''

''Jesus,'' Jarvis said, rolling his eyes ceilingward. ''I hope you're going to manage to take this seriously while the clock's running.''

''I hope I manage not to,'' Reynolds said cheerily. ''Let's go have some fun, boys. Shrike season opens today.''

Bhodi's team called itself the Immortals, but in the first match they looked very mortal indeed. Right from the opening, they had trouble matching the energy level of the Shrikes, who came out of their end with a furious five-man attack. Shortly thereafter, Waverly and White were taken in by a diversion and surrendered a hit on their base goal—this before two minutes had gone by.

For his own part, Bhodi felt himself pressing, and neither his anticipation nor his shooting was as sharp as usual.

More than once he crossed paths with Duane at inopportune times, ruining a stalk or ambush. And not once, but four times did he suffer through the electronic raspberry that meant he'd been fried by one of the Shrikes.

Halfway through the match, the Immortals collected themselves and clawed their way back to an even footing with the Shrikes. The lead changed seven times in the last frantic minute, with the eventual winning shot coming not from Bhodi's phaser, but from Reynolds'. A moment before the lights came up, he scored against a Shrike huddled in a hidey-hole as though trying to run out the clock.

"That was fun for the people upstairs," a breathless Dennis Waverly said afterward, "but let's not have any more of them, okay?"

It didn't need saying. The close call seemed to bring them together, and in their second match they had a three-hundred point margin after three minutes and never gave the other team a chance to whittle it down. In their third match, they eliminated the tournament's only all-girl team in a low-scoring seesaw battle in which neither team reached the other's base goal.

That put them in the championship match against the Panzer Boys, a team of six men in their twenties whose progress through the tournament Jarvis and his teammates had noted with growing respect. During the long break between the semifinals and the championship, they sat together around a table in the center's snack bar and sipped at cold drinks. Most were looking ahead, but Jarvis could not stop looking back.

"I don't know what's wrong," he moped. "I haven't been over twelve hundred points all day. I just can't seem to get in the flow."

"I know. This team play is killing you," Reynolds said, and looked around the circle. "New plan, okay? Greg, Dennis, Robert, you run a three-man defense—like hockey,

goalie and two defensemen. Brian, you take sniper duty."
He looked back at Jarvis. "You and I will work a pair,
like you talked about yesterday—remember?"

"That's what we should have been doing all day."

Reynolds smiled wisely. "And if we had, the Panzer
Boys would have had a chance to study us and figure out
how to handle it."

"Ah—" said White, understanding.

"So forget we're here," Reynolds continued. "Find the
flow. I'll protect your back. Think about the record, if
that's what it takes."

Duane threw his hands in the air. "That's all we need.
Look, we've been winning, haven't we?"

"No, just a minute," White said. "I think David's got
something. These guys have chewed 2-2-2's up all day."

"They haven't been up against ours," Morse said, leaning back in his chair with his arms across his chest.

"Look, if you don't want to do it that way, it's no skin
off my behind," Reynolds said. "I only thought—"

"David's right," Jarvis said quietly. "I've been fighting
myself all day trying to be a team player, taking that extra
moment to try to sync what I'm about to do with whoever
was nearby. It just isn't my way. Let's do it David's way.
You'll all come out of it even, or even a couple hundred
down a man. I'll get us the margin we need."

Jarvis was so collected and determined that there was no
further argument. Instead, Morse glanced at his watch and
stood up from the table.

"Time to go back," he said. "Let's do it. Let's get
'em."

Even before the match began, Jarvis knew how it would
come out. Standing in the runway waiting to be called into
the arena for introductions, he systematically shut himself
off from the distracting stimuli and recaptured the clean

focus of his early morning meditation. If he had been interrupted, he could not have said exactly what it was that he was thinking. He only knew that when the Klaxon sounded, he was ready.

And from the very beginning, the transformation was complete and miraculous. Bhodi Li ran, spun, dove, rolled, pounced. His attack was reckless, and his out-of-control style played havoc with the Panzer Boys' deliberate, structured strategy.

With Reynolds providing unacknowledged and often unrecognized help, Jarvis ambushed their ambushes, stalked their scouts, and picked off their snipers. He appeared behind them as they cautiously approached what they thought was his hiding place. When he could, he challenged an opponent's reflexes in the open floor, one on one, and usually came out best.

By the four-minute mark, the outcome of the match was no longer in doubt. The Panzer Boys had twice retreated in disarray to their base to regroup. The second time their discussion sounded more like a fractious argument, and when they came out that time, it was with a noticeable lack of enthusiasm.

The only remaining question was whether Bhodi Li could break Evan Kyley's arena record. As his total climbed past 2000, the game operator posted the record on the main scoreboard, and the audience in the gallery suddenly came alive.

"Bhodi, Bhodi, Bhodi!" The chant started with a half-dozen of Jarvis's friends and quickly spread through the gallery. Hearing it, two of the Panzer Boys started falling back toward their base goals as though they had at last found something to motivate them—denying Bhodi Li the base and the record.

Jarvis was aware of their movements, but only subconsciously aware of the crowd. Before the reinforcements could reach cover in front of the base, Jarvis burst from the alcove and surprised them from the side. He took out both on the run and dove into a shoulder roll that brought him directly in front of the base and its lone defender. Whipping his phaser up to eye level, he squeezed off two quick shots, ending the duel before it could begin.

Bouncing to his feet, Jarvis advanced on the base, savoring the moment, raising his weapon with triumphant deliberateness. Now he heard the chanting of his warrior name, the heavy rhythmic clapping from above somehow one with the thrumming of his own racing heart.

This is the way it's supposed to feel, he thought, and squeezed the trigger three times. The base's lights flashed to confirm the hit, and on the scoreboard high above, Bhodi Li's score changed to 2520. Instantly, the cheers crescendoed to a roar, a roar that drowned out the music.

But in the next moment, everything changed. The roar was suddenly choked off, and all Jarvis could hear was a sound like a dozen operatic voices singing a dozen different floating melodies all at once. He smacked the side of his helmet with the flat of his hand, but the eerie chorus continued.

Spinning around, he looked at the enemy guards, and David standing beyond them. They all seemed to be frozen in place. One of the guards was scowling and toeing the ramp. The mouth of another Panzer Boy was puckered as though he were about to spit on the floor in disgust. David's hands were caught in mid-clap, his joyful grin as unchanging as though he were a marble statue.

Beyond the immobile figures, the arena was fast growing darker, and the remaining light was taking on a bluish cast. Jarvis turned back toward the goal and found it radiating a bizarre metallic blue light, like a neon floodlamp. The glow was spreading from the center to engulf the entire goal, and as it spread, the music grew louder.

He could not find his voice to plead for help or demand

explanations. All he could do is stand, transfixed, as the blue light suddenly exploded from its source and swirled around him like a million Day-Glo fireflies. The swarm blended into a cloud so dense he could not see beyond it, then contracted into a blue light cocoon that held him gently but firmly in its embrace.

When at last the cocoon released him and faded away, the arena, his teammates, his family, everything that had surrounded him in the moment before the cheering stopped, was gone.

CHAPTER 4

Jarvis was alone in a silent, empty chamber twice his height and three armspans wide. That he was *somewhere else* he knew without question. It was more than the evidence of his eyes. The very air had changed. The ceiling glowed with a diffused bluish light, as though it were a residue of the cocoon that had hidden from him the means and moment of his translocation.

He stood there in the middle of the chamber paralyzed as thoroughly as his friends in the arena had been, paralyzed by confusion and not a little fear. His mind could not begin to manufacture explanations for what had happened. Even the feeble thought that this was some sort of trick cooked up by the Center for the tournament was almost behind him.

"David?" he croaked, a slight tremor of panic in his voice.

There was no answer. He was alone.

But he was not alone for long.

The walls, floor, and ceiling were flawless and unbroken. He had begun to wonder how he had been brought into the room, and was on the verge of wondering how he would get out. Then a pinpoint of light appeared at eye level in the middle of the wall Jarvis was facing. The pinpoint grew rapidly into a white diamond-shaped hole in the wall, which kept expanding until the bottom point reached the floor and the opening was large enough to be called a doorway.

A moment later, while Jarvis was still marveling, a short black-skinned human boy wearing a battered Philadelphia Phillies baseball cap stepped through the opening, smiled and said, quite casually, "Hello, Chris."

Jarvis swallowed hard, then found his voice. "What's going on here?"

"Someone else will be coming in a few moments from now to answer that question," the boy said in a precise and cultured voice that was at odds with his apparent age, about ten. He reached out and handed Jarvis a small rubber-and-metal plug, slightly larger than the eraser on a pencil. "Place that in your right ear canal, please. It's an interlingual translator and you will need what it does in just a few moments."

Stunned beyond resistance, Bhodi numbly complied. To his surprise, the translator did not interfere the least with his hearing.

"My name is Parcival," the boy went on. "Like you, I'm from Earth. I want to assure you that despite any apprehension you might be feeling, you're in no danger—"

"I'm not afraid."

"If you say so," Parcival said politely. "The important thing is that you remain calm and listen carefully to everything that you're told—"

With a rush, Jarvis's mental logjam began breaking up. "*From* Earth," he sputtered. "A stupid thing—why would you say—of course you're *from* Earth! There's nowhere else to be from—"

His voice trailed off as a great bulk moved into the doorway, blocking the light streaming through. Moving on two legs stout enough to have belonged to century-old birch trees, the inhuman figure stepped through the opening.

Jarvis gaped. In size and appearance both, it was a monster, all teeth and scarred scaly skin and huge oval eyes. With its head thrust forward like a lizard, Jarvis could see the beginning of a line of rounded spines starting at its nape and continuing down its back. A thick muscular tail lashed back and forth slowly, the tip brushing the floor of the chamber with a sound like a straw broom on concrete.

What it was, where it could be from—these were unfathomable mysteries. But the thing that puzzled Jarvis even more was that the beast was wearing what could only be called fatigues, sleeves rolled up to the elbow, legs tucked into thick-soled black boots. On the beast's right shoulder was some sort of insignia in electric blue and gold; strapped to its right calf was a brown-handled throwing knife in a scabbard.

"As you're starting to realize, there are many subjects on which you're not fully educated," Parcival said with a sympathetic smile. "Christopher Jarvis, may I introduce Nar-lex-ko-li-hon, Sergeant of the Ninth Platoon of the Guardians of Light—and a true Photon Warrior."

Jarvis stared at the alien, then at Parcival, then back at the alien. "I don't believe any of this," he said. "I was in the Photon Center, playing a match—"

"This isn't play, Bhodi Li," Li-hon said. "The Photon—"

"You speak English!"

"You hear English," Li-hon corrected.

This time Jarvis saw that the alien's stiff lips and dancing tongue moved like in a badly synchronized movie. Whatever sounds it really was making, he could not hear. If it's making any sounds at all—

"I'm not buying it," Jarvis said, shaking his head. "That's a costume, and this is some kind of trick. I don't know what you did to me in the Center, but it's not enough to make me think that anything like you can be real."

"Where do you think you are, Chris?" Parcival asked before Li-hon could respond.

"I don't know," Jarvis said, throwing his hands in the air. "Somewhere in the Center. A back room somewhere."

"Would you like to go out through the door with me and see where you are?"

A little tremor of doubt ran through Jarvis. "Yeah. Yeah, I'd like that just fine," he said nevertheless.

"Li-hon?" Parcival said as though asking permission.

"This is not the customary procedure."

"He has to know, or we'll get nowhere. I warned you about that."

"Very well," the creature agreed. "I will meet you in the chart room after."

"Done. Come with me, Chris," Parcival said, turning and leading the way.

Outside the chamber, Jarvis found himself following the boy down a wide corridor that reminded him of the tunnel in his high school between the boiler and utility rooms. Brightly colored tubes and conduits masked much of the ceiling. Some were transparent, with a viscous blue-green liquid bubbling through them. Some had side branches that came down the walls to what looked like high-tech fuse boxes with five-by-five grids of glowing lights.

But even though he could connect what he was to things he knew, nothing he saw really looked familiar. "Are we in the basement?" he asked hopefully.

"No," Parcival said, stopping at what seemed to be a blank spot in the right wall. He touched his hand to a diamond-shaped panel, and the wall opened up into another doorway. Glancing back first to see that Jarvis was with him, Parcival stepped through.

"I want to know how you do that," Jarvis said, dogging the boy's heels. Then he stopped short, and his mouth went dry. The cylindrical room they had entered had a window—a wide slab of glass that divided the far wall in half.

Except it couldn't be glass, because the view out the window was of the Earth.

It was the Earth as he had never seen it, from hundreds of miles up: land and sea and cloud all gliding by beneath him like a NASA film come to life. Parallel streamers of clouds like white furrows cut across the sky, echoed by shadows on the multihued brown landscape. The light-colored shallows and sand bars showed up clearly against the darker ocean depths.

"This is nuts," Jarvis muttered.

"I hope you understand now—"

"I'm on a spaceship? In orbit?"

"Yes—a scoutship belonging to the Photon Alliance," Parcival said. "You were brought here from the Photon Center by a spacetime transporter link."

"But things like this aren't real!" Jarvis protested.

"You're being dense," Parcival said impatiently. "Look around you. Look out there. Don't you believe what you see? Would you rather believe you're crazy? Or that we're tricksters?"

"But what's it all about?"

"Sergeant Li-hon is waiting to tell you—if you're ready to listen."

Jarvis looked away from Parcival and down on the Earth. It was all ocean underneath them now except for a string of three islands, each ringed by its own pale green atoll and capped by tiny white cloud puffs.

It was real. It could be nothing but. And if it was real, then he was where Parcival said he was, and—hard as it was to accept—Li-hon was what he seemed to be.

"I guess I'm ready to listen."

Parcival smiled and clapped Jarvis on the shoulder familiarly. "I knew you'd be okay. Come on, then. Li-hon is waiting."

"Just a minute. If this is all what it seems, what are you doing here? What's your relationship to the big lizard? Are you a prisoner or something? A toady?"

Parcival laughed unexpectedly, and only then did Jarvis realize his pun. "I'm a Photon Warrior," the youth said. "Sergeant Li-hon is my commander."

"*You're* a Photon Warrior?"

"Yes."

Jarvis shook his head. "Nothing personal, but there must not be much to getting in, then."

Parcival's expression darkened. "It's lucky for you that it's me you said that to," he said tersely. "If you'd said it to nine out of ten Warriors, they'd have used the floor or the nearest bulkhead to wipe the smirk off your face. If you were lucky, by the time they'd satisfied their honor, you'd only have a few broken bones. Me, I'm not that sensitive to ignorant comments. If somebody's dumb enough to think that just because I'm smaller than them I couldn't possibly be a danger to them, that's fine—it gives me that much more edge if I ever have to kill them."

Jarvis stared. "You mean it, don't you?"

"Every word. Now come on—the sergeant's waiting."

Parcival led Jarvis to a six-sided compartment full of unfathomable electronics consoles. The one object Jarvis recognized by its function was the small hexagonal table at which the alien sat.

"Is he ready?" Li-hon asked Parcival.

"I think so," the boy said, settling onto an open stool on the nearest side of the table.

That left Jarvis the only one standing. He looked from Parcival to Li-hon questioningly.

"Sit down, Bhodi Li," the sergeant said in answer to the look. He waited a moment until Jarvis had complied, then went on: "Bhodi Li, as we sit here talking, there is fighting on seventeen worlds between the Guardians of Light and the forces of the Arrian Alliance. It is a struggle that threatens all civilized worlds, including your own Earth."

"Do you mean that there's seventeen planets out there with life on them? Seventeen different kinds of life?"

"For the most part, the fighting has been confined to uninhabited worlds. In fact, it may be said that those worlds are what the fighting's about. But if the Arrians gain the advantage there, no one doubts that they will carry the fight to the homeworlds of Light. And there are many more than seventeen homeworlds. There are, in fact, ninety."

Jarvis glanced sideways at Parcival. "Is this on the level?"

"We didn't bring you here to lie to you," Parcival said.

"Maybe—maybe not. Who knows about this?" Jarvis asked. "NASA? The government?"

"No one," Li-hon said. "No one but those who have displayed sufficient skill to be considered for a place among the honored Guardians. You have been thinking of Photon as a game, and for those of average skill it will never be more than that. But for those with special gifts, it is an audition. The game is played, with variations appropriate to the native technologies, on—how many, Parcival?"

"Twenty-eight," the youth supplied.

"On twenty-eight worlds. Each time a player of promise enters the arena, his efforts there are recorded and studied—"

"And when they get good enough, you recruit them?"

"That's why we are here, Bhodi Li," Li-hon said. "To

offer you the honor of challenging for a place among us and the glory of contributing to the defense of your homeworld.''

''Me?''

''Why are you surprised? Haven't you boasted that there is no one who is better in the arena than you?''

''But that's completely different—''

''Are you refusing the honor offered?''

''I'm just trying to understand,'' Jarvis protested. ''If you've got so many worlds, why do you recruit from places that don't even know the war exists? Can't you get enough from the homeworlds?''

''The kind of war we're fighting isn't anything like in the twentieth century,'' Parcival said. ''It's more like a medieval combat where both sides send out their champions and everybody else sits on the sidelines and drinks mead. There's no mass armies, not yet anyway.''

''Then I'm even more confused. If you only need a few soldiers, why can't you find them inside the—what did you call it, the Photon Alliance?''

Parcival said, ''Every species has something special to contribute. And the more resources the First Guardian has to call on, the stronger we are.''

''The First Guardian—what is that, your president, or king or something?''

''The First Guardian is the supreme commander of the Guardians of Light, to whom Parcival and I have both sworn our service and allegiance,'' said the alien. ''To complete the answer to your last question, there is also a matter of honor.''

''Honor? What's honor got to do with it?''

''The First Guardian knows that to announce our existence to Earth would cause great shock and disarray. But the First Guardian also knows that if Earth did have full knowledge of the crisis, it would insist on contributing to its own defense. This way, we are not responsible for Earth experiencing either the pain of learning or the shame of life obligation,'' Li-hon said.

''If that's what you're trying to do, you're not as smart as you think you are,'' Jarvis said. ''You kidnapped me in front of hundreds of people. You may have had a secret, but you sure don't now.''

Parcival smiled in silent amusement as Li-hon answered. ''If you refuse the honor, the device that brought you here is capable of replacing you at the instant you were, as you call it, kidnapped,'' the alien said. ''You will remember nothing, and you will never have been missed.'' He hesitated, then added, ''Now we have answered enough questions. It is time for you to decide.''

''Not so fast,'' Jarvis said sharply. ''Okay, so if I say 'No thank you,' I go back. What happens if I accept? Does that make me a Photon Warrior?''

''No,'' Parcival said. ''That's only the beginning.''

''No one becomes a Photon Warrior without passing through the Three Refusals,'' Li-hon said. ''Three times, you will be asked to give up your challenge. After the first refusal, your education will begin. After the second, your training. After the third, your service. Only then will you be a Photon Warrior. Only then do you become a Guardian of the Light. If you fail at any point, or give up your challenge, you will be returned to Earth just as we have already described.''

''And until then, what's happening at home? Time doesn't stop for them.''

''No,'' Parcival said. ''The timeline proceeds for them. But nothing's real, and nothing's permanent. When the transporter replaces you in their past, the Universe itself will edit out the invalidated events. Don't expect to understand it now.''

''Enough,'' Li-hon said. ''Bhodi Li, you have earned

on merit the right to challenge for a place among the Guardians of Light. Will you give up your challenge?''

Jarvis looked at Parcival, then at Nar-lex-ko-li-hon. *What a choice,* he thought. *If I say yes, I'm out of this free, without even any memory of it to make me feel like I chickened out. If I say no, I can go to the stars—but only as a soldier-in-training for a war that I've got no stake in. Or no stake that I can see, anyway. What a choice—but what a chance—*

"No," he said firmly. "I won't give up my challenge."

Parcival smiled and raised a clenched fist, while Li-hon nodded approvingly. "Parcival will show you your quarters," the sergeant said, rising up on his powerful legs. "We'll get underway as soon as the flight checks are complete."

CHAPTER 5

En route to the crew quarters, Jarvis learned that the ship was named *Fraanic*. Parcival explained that a fraanic was a small tree-living creature from a world in the Sadr system.

"It screams bloody murder when a predator comes near," Parcival said. "It makes a sound kind of like a cat being put in a blender tail-first."

"How would you know what that sounds like? Or maybe I shouldn't ask."

"It's just an analogy," Parcival said impatiently. "I *like* cats. Anyway, it makes a perfect name for a scoutship, don't you think?"

"You have bigger ships?"

"Oh, sure," was the cheerful reply. "The Alliance classes ships by the size of the fractional drive they carry. We're running under a one-mass—as small as they come. Our platoon's assault ship, the *Zephyr*, has a three-mass. The biggest ships we ever use run a six, though there're civilian freighters and general carriers out of Foppo that go as high as an eight."

"Seems like what you'd want to do is jack up a scout with an eight and get there that much faster."

Parcival shook his head. "It doesn't work that way. This ship is just as fast as a carrier with an eight-mass. The only difference favors this ship—its quicker, more agile."

"Because it's smaller?"

The youth started down a ladderway. "Because it has less mass," he called back over his shoulder. "Do you know any tensor calculus? If you do, I can explain it all to you in ten minutes."

Jarvis followed him down. "No. I barely passed Introduction to Trigonometry."

Waiting for him at the bottom, Parcival looked disappointed. "Oh, well. In that case, I couldn't explain it to you in ten years." He gestured at the new surroundings. "Are you lost yet?"

"Not quite."

"The layout of the ship is really pretty simple—unless you need to go into the tech crawlways. The upper deck has the transporter chamber, the chart room, the bridge, the mapping and sensor stations. Downstairs there are all the personal areas—berths and galley and such. That's my quarters there," Parcival said, pointing at what looked like a blank wall.

"I think I've got it—except I have trouble spotting the doorways."

"Look for the touchplates. The doorways are always to the right."

"Must have been designed by lefties."

"As a matter of fact, the race that builds these is exclusively left-handed. You know, you're taking this all very well," Parcival said approvingly as he led Jarvis to the end of the corridor. "You wouldn't happen to be a science fiction fan, would you?"

"You mean, like, books?"

"Sure. Heinlein—Asimov—Silverberg—Doc Smith."

Jarvis shook his head. "No. I don't read much." Then

he added, "But I've seen the Bud Light space station commercial a lot."

Parcival chortled and reached out to a touchplate on the right wall. "In here," he said as the doorway appeared.

The cabin was no larger than a walk-in closet even before Parcival showed Jarvis how to fold down the cot and unfold the collapsed storage bins. "Sergeant Li-hon couldn't turn around in here, much less relax," Jarvis said. "Are all the cabins this small?"

"Yes and no. The sergeant has a double-wide. And the cabins are modular—the shipwrights can customize the space to the species that are going to be aboard. This is a standard human berth. Mine's just like it."

"How many people are on this ship?"

"*Fraanic* can accommodate eight. But you've already seen everyone who's aboard."

"You and Li-hon are the whole crew?"

"You're thinking about this all wrong. You wouldn't say the family car had a crew, would you?"

"Do you mean flying this thing across the galaxy isn't any harder than driving the Buick to the grocery?"

"Actually, it's easier."

"Who's the pilot? Li-hon? Or you?"

"The ship is," Parcival said, edging toward the door. "Nothing personal, Chris, but you've played four matches today without a shower. Why don't you take some time to check out the washrooms and then come on back upstairs? There are fresh coveralls in the washroom locker. You can leave your Photon gear in the storeall there. You won't be needing it."

Jarvis frowned. "I'd like to watch us leave orbit. How long until we get under way?"

"We're already under way."

"But I didn't feel anything—"

"Why did you expect to? It's the fractional drive that's

moving us, not a reaction engine. No rocket that's ever been invented would get us where we're going in less than a thousand years. And if anything faster had been invented, we'd be splattered over the aft bulkheads the first time we lit it up. We're not going to the moon, Chris—our destination's nineteen light-years away."

"Nineteen light-years," Jarvis repeated. "I have no idea how far that is. How long will it take us to get there?"

Parcival smiled. "A little less than two days."

A distracted look came onto Jarvis's face, and he nodded in absent acknowledgment. Parcival turned away and slapped the touchplate familiarly.

"Parcival?"

The youth looked back.

"Why do you call me Chris, but he calls me Bhodi Li?"

"Because I understand that your Photon name is something you put on and take off with your gear. Because Bhodi Li happens to be a warrior name in his language. Why'd you pick that name, anyway? It doesn't mean anything in English."

"No. I made it up. I wanted something sort of exotic sounding, Oriental—like a kung fu name." He hesitated. "What does it mean to Li-hon?"

Parcival studied Jarvis for a long moment before answering. "Battle-child."

"Battle-child," he repeated. "Okay. I'll be up in a little while."

"Okay," Parcival said, turning away again.

"Parcival?"

"What?"

"I think maybe it'd be simpler if you called me Bhodi Li, too."

Parcival frowned disapprovingly, then shrugged. "If that's what you want—Bhodi Li."

The doorway contracted behind him, leaving Jarvis alone with the disquieting sense that Parcival understood something about him that he himself did not.

Why should he care what name I use? It doesn't mean anything either way—

But it did mean something. It had pleased him to hear the alien call him by his Photon name and pleased him even more to learn that chance had given that name appropriate meaning.

He knew that there was a clue in that which could tell him what had troubled the youth, but Bhodi Li could not read it. So he did what he had always done when understanding escaped him—he dismissed the matter from his mind. He wanted a shower, and then he wanted more answers—many more answers. The moratorium on questions had ended when he proclaimed his first refusal, and Bhodi Li intended to take full advantage of his freedom while it lasted.

It was the strangest shower Bhodi Li had ever taken. There was no shower head; when he touched the controls inside the bathing enclosure, droplets of lukewarm water began to fall from the entire surface of the ceiling as though he were standing outside in a drizzle. There was no way to shower and not wash one's hair at the same time; in fact, there was no place Bhodi Li could stand and not have water running down his face and into his eyes.

Further fiddling increased the intensity of the falling water to that of a summer squall, but if there were a way to alter the temperature, Bhodi Li never found it. *Maybe that's the point*, he thought. *Maybe in the rest of the galaxy they only wash when it rains.*

There were no towels and no obvious substitutes, like a blower or radiator. Bhodi Li eventually used one pair of coveralls to dry off before climbing into a second pair. The wet garment went with his fragrant arena clothes into a receptacle that Bhodi Li hoped was a hamper and not some other species' version of a toilet.

Returning to the upper deck, Bhodi Li made his way down the corridor compartment by compartment, less to look for the others than to cement his mental picture of the ship's plan. He understood little of what he saw but made himself remember enough to distinguish one room from another.

He found Li-hon and Parcival both in the relatively spacious arrowhead-shaped compartment at the end of the corridor. But he paid almost no attention to them. His attention was captured by the three broad rectangular windows—right, left and center—inset above the U-shaped bridge console.

The two side windows were pure black, telling Bhodi Li that they were not windows at all but some sort of video display. But the forward window was alive with streaks of reddish light radiating outward from a central focus; it looked as though *Fraanic* were diving through an exploding fireworks shell.

"What makes the stars look like that?" Bhodi Li asked, pointing.

"Those aren't the stars," Parcival said tolerantly. "We're traveling too fast to see anything but tachyons, except there turns out to be no such thing."

"Then what is that?"

"Harl-ben-qi-jaslan," Li-hon said. "The Female Wept Twice."

"What?"

"It's a poem Li-hon is working on," Parcival said. "One of his better ones, too."

"Flattery won't change your duty load," Li-hon said.

"A poem?" was Bhodi Li's skeptical reply. "A poem is 'How do I love thee?,' or maybe 'There once was a lady from Kent—' "

"This is a color poem," Li-hon said. "Very popular on Bree-nech."

"But there's no words."

"It is meant to stimulate the mind directly," said Li-hon.

Bhodi Li watched the changing patterns for a few seconds. "I'm not getting anything."

"You have to learn how to open yourself," Li-hon said, unperturbed. "But if you never learn, don't worry. I write word poems, too."

Bhodi Li turned a quizzical look on the alien. "Isn't that a little strange, for someone who looks like you—a Guardian of the Light—to write poetry?"

"On your world, do warriors only know how to kill?"

"Well—no, I guess not. But they find other ways to spend their spare time."

"Cultivate the whole," Li-hon said, sounding like some sort of golden-oldie guru. "If you define yourself by what you do, you will lose sight of what you are."

"Sure," Bhodi Li said noncommittally. Silently, he was thinking, a kid warrior and a sergeant that spends his spare time writing poems you have to watch—the First Guardian must be harder up for good people than they're letting me think. Or maybe these are just the First Guardian's errand boys, and the front-line troops are cut from different cloth. "When are you going to tell me what this war is all about?"

"Are you ready for the Truth of Photon?" Li-hon asked.

"Sure."

"Then sit, Bhodi Li, and learn."

The lights dimmed on the bridge as the color poem vanished from the center window, leaving the compartment in darkness. "Before time, before light, before life, there was Photon," Li-hon said, and a swirling ball of blue-white light appeared behind him. "In simplicity and completeness, Photon contained all energy, embraced all of space, embodied all order. There was balance, but there was also stasis. So, to gift the universe with growth and change, Photon chose—''

''That thing's alive?'' Bhodi Li said.

From Parcival, seated behind, came a harsh whisper: ''Don't interrupt.''

''—chose to spread its essence throughout creation. Order ended, and time began.''

The ball of swirling light suddenly exploded, sending rocket like streamers out in every direction, filling all three windows with color. ''Where the energy of Photon touched the new creation, stars and planets formed,'' Li-hon continued as the streamers of color evolved into a more familiar-looking starscape full of flaming suns and slow-spinning worlds. ''In time, Photon light brought forth Photon life. Born from Photon, we held within us the truth of Photon, and so brought the light to other worlds.''

The center window showed a pulsing many-faceted crystal resting on a black pedestal on the surface of a barren world. A Qeth warrior, perhaps Li-hon himself, fired a laser into the heart of the crystal, and it exploded into a furious mass of colored light reminiscent of the destruction of the primordial Photon energy ball. The streaming colored light transformed the barren world into a verdant paradise.

''But there was darkness in the new creation as well, and in time the darkness, too, gave birth to life,'' Li-hon continued. On the center screen, the new world of life faded and was replaced by a succession of shocking images of horrifying aliens—a four-armed monster with a deeply furrowed skull, a snarling beast with huge jaws and spiked tail, a brutish creature with a triangular head and great bulging compound eyes.

Bhodi Li swallowed hard. *If they're the enemy, you can take me home now—*

"The forces of darkness have united under the Warlord of Arr, and begun the battle that will decide the destiny of the universe. It is a battle for control of the remnants of Photon energy, and for the Photon crystals that bring light and life to empty worlds. Whoever radiates the crystal first aligns that world with light or darkness for the next hundred cycles. Should the forces of evil bring a crystal to one of the Alliance worlds—to my Bree-nech or your Earth or any world dear to life—it would mean the destruction of all."

On the left screen, an image of a great space station appeared against a backdrop of stars, its shape suggestive of a metallic flower perched at the top of its stalk. On the right screen, a radically different structure appeared against a black void, its shape like an A-bomb cloud frozen a moment after detonation, its surface battered and scarred like the moon. Tiny ships scurried from both bases to engage each other above the worlds displayed on the center screen.

"If the Alliance loses this conflict, it will be the end of light and life everywhere in the Universe," Li-hon said solemnly. "Do you understand now, Bhodi Li? We are Photon's warriors. We are the Guardians of the Light. We cannot let the darkness grow."

All three screens faded to black, and the bridge lights returned to their normal intensity. Bhodi Li stayed seated, his arms crossed over his chest, his gaze cast downward at the deck. *How stupid does he think I am?* he thought angrily. *Balls of light deciding to explode—magic crystals that turn deserts into Eden—creatures of darkness—it's a fairy tale. It's a crock.*

"Do you understand, Bhodi Li?" Li-hon repeated. Looking up, he saw an expectant gaze on the lizard's face. Parcival had circled around to stand beside his sergeant; curiously, his expression was harder to read.

"I thought you were going to be straight with me," Bhodi Li said, standing.

Suddenly wide-eyed, Parcival stepped back, taking himself beyond Li-hon's peripheral vision, and started frantically shaking his head.

"Every word I spoke was the truth," Li-hon said stiffly.

"Get real! You can't expect me to swallow—" Belatedly, Bhodi Li took note of Parcival's agitation. The youth now had one hand clapped over his mouth and was making cutting motions across his throat with the other.

What? Bhodi Li demanded silently with his eyes. *What am I doing wrong?* Then he remembered Parcival's earlier warning about offending a Photon Warrior and decided to swallow his objections for the moment. "You can't expect me to adjust right away to such a revelation," Bhodi Li said. "I need some time to absorb this."

Parcival closed his eyes and sighed in relief.

But Li-hon did not seem willing to be put off. "The truth was already within you," he said. "All you need do is learn its name to be empowered by it."

It was Parcival who came to his rescue. "I'll help him, Li-hon. Don't be impatient. It's difficult for us—you've seen it before. We don't hear with the heart. So it takes longer for us to find the light."

"I know," Li-hon said ominously. "I remember. Some never do."

Parcival left Li-hon's side and crossed the room, herding Bhodi Li ahead of him toward the doorway. "Bhodi will," he insisted. "The light shines."

"The light shines," echoed Li-hon. "I will be patient, Parcival—for a while."

CHAPTER 6

"What was that all about?" Bhodi Li demanded as Parcival bundled him along the corridor.

"Let it ride until we get downstairs," was the terse answer. Then Parcival changed gears and said in a more friendly tone, "I hope you don't have any exotic tastes in food, by the way. The ground team prepares a food pickup anytime a ship calls at Earth, but the selection's limited, and most everything is frozen. Except the peanut butter."

By the end of that exposition, they had both reached the bottom of the climbway. "I suppose that means it's going to be a while until my next pizza."

"Until your next good one, anyway."

"If it gets to be more than a week, even a cardboard-crusted imitation-cheese-food special will start looking good," Bhodi Li said. "Do I get an answer to my question now?"

"Let's go sit a minute in my quarters," the youth said with a jerk of his head.

Parcival's berth was a case study in how much could be packed into one of the tiny rooms, especially if the occupant happened to be only four feet tall and sixty-five pounds. The right-hand wall was broken up by six fold-out storealls, each the size of the one Parcival had opened in Bhodi Li's room. Above the storealls hung several soft-sided pouches bulging with their burdens. The cot was folded down, and the space beneath it was filled with large silver-metal chests. A baseball bat was propped in one corner, a well-used glove dangling from the grip.

Bhodi settled on the cot while Parcival climbed atop one of the storealls and rummaged in the pouch above it. He came back with a matchbox-sized black box that he stood on end beside him. A small yellow light on top of the gadget began to wink on and off.

"It's a sound mask. Li-hon wouldn't spy on us, but I want to make sure he doesn't hear any of this by accident," Parcival explained.

"I don't understand."

"That's obvious. I can hardly believe it, but you're even dumber than you look. Haven't you got sense enough not to stand in somebody else's church and make fun of the liturgy?" Parcival scolded.

"What are you talking about?"

"I'm talking about what you were about to say to the Sarge a few minutes ago."

"You heard the line he was giving me. Don't tell me you believe him."

Parcival sighed and pulled his legs up into a yoga lotus cross as though settling in for a while. "You were in school twice as long as I was, and you still didn't learn anything."

A hot flush crept up the back of Bhodi's neck. "Hey, I've had about enough of your smart talk. Maybe you are some kind of born genius, but that doesn't make it okay to dump on people that aren't."

Parcival stared, then hung his head. "You're right," he said simply. "I get impatient with people who are slow on the uptake. I always have. I'll try to watch it."

"Okay," Bhodi said, taken aback by the youth's contriteness. He noticed that his own fists were clenched and unclenched them, wondering in passing if Parcival had backed off to avoid having to fight him—and if there was anything to his boasting, having to hurt him. "So let's try it again."

"All right," Parcival said. "Do you know what the word photon means?"

"Uh—it's got something to do with light. Wait, isn't it the little particles light is made of?"

"More or less. The photon is the fundamental unit of radiant energy. To these people it's something even more fundamental than that. They've personified and deified light into the First Principle of the cosmos. What you heard from Li-hon is what's called a cosmogony—an explanation of the origin of things. By the way, what's yours?"

"What's my what?"

"What's your explanation for the existence of stars and human beings and peanut butter?"

Bhodi Li struggled to dredge up some scraps of abandoned memory. "Well—in science they told us something about the big bang. And then a few million years later there were these little water animals in the ocean and then evolution took over—dinosaurs, and Neanderthals, and then us. There were ice ages, too. Peanut butter was George Washington Carver," he added with a grin.

"I don't think I've ever heard it compressed quite that ruthlessly," Parcival said, answering the grin with a wry smile. "And your time scale is off by a factor of a thousand. What about God?"

"Well—that's another story. How does the creed go? 'I believe in God the Father, maker of heaven and earth and of all things visible and invisible'—something like that."

"So answer my question. What's your explanation? What do *you* believe?"

Bhodi Li was beginning to feel like he was taking an oral exam. "Well—I guess I believe that the big bang was when God started everything. And everything that happened after was part of His plan. You know, evolution was His way of making us. I don't guess I've really thought about it much."

"Typical," Parcival sniffed, with a hint of his earlier condescension. "So what you believe is a mixture of facts and guesses and things you take on authority, like the idea there even is a God, and they don't necessarily fit together smoothly. Just like what you heard from Li-hon."

"Are you saying that what I believe would sound as cracked to Li-hon as what he said did to me?"

"It might. But if it did, he'd be being as unfair as you were going to be to him." Parcival paused to collect his thoughts. "To Li-hon, to the whole Alliance as far as I can tell, what he told you isn't a religious belief. It's the way they look at the Universe. It's part of what they are. They accept it as unquestioningly as we accept breathing and eating and sleeping when it's dark."

"But they *are* wrong."

Shaking his head, Parcival said, "They're like the old human societies that worshiped the sun as God the lifegiver. They weren't all wrong. And neither is Li-hon. But it does affect how they look at the war. It may even be the reason for the war."

"Really? How?"

"Would you like to hear the Gospel according to Parcival? I haven't got it all figured out, but I've got a pretty interesting working hypothesis."

"Can we get something to eat first?"

Parcival hopped off his perch. "Good idea."

"I know it is," Bhodi Li said. "Even we morons have them every now and then."

Over a surprisingly good cheeseburger with a fresh Red Delicious apple on the side, Bhodi Li listened attentively to Parcival's version of the Photon cosmogony.

According to Parcival, it began with a race called the Ylem. To them, the big bang was not an act of God—it was the creator God itself, giving up its own life to bring life to the Universe. The stars were remnants of God in its purest form; the life-forms populating the planets the fulfillment of God's final wish.

When the Ylem became spacefaring they also became evangelists, carrying the Truth of Photon to the other inhabited worlds. With their starships and other technological miracles to validate their status as special messengers of revelation, they brought answers to beings which up to that point had only questions. The Alliance was forged on the strength of the Ylem cosmogony.

But unifying all known life in one belief was not enough to satisfy the Alliance's sense of mission. To the Ylem and their converts, it seemed not fitting that there should be stars with no life of their own. They saw it as their holy obligation to colonize one world in every system, thereby helping to complete their Creator's final vision. Where there were no planets suitable for habitation, they made one over with the help of the Photon crystals.

"They regard them almost as religious artifacts, like the Eucharist or a piece of the Shroud of Turin," Parcival explained. "But they're really tremendous little chemical laboratories driven by microfusion and solar energy. What they do is modify a planet's atmosphere so it supports our kind of life."

"That sounds as much like magic as what Li-hon showed me."

"Oh, not at all. The elements that you need are almost always present on the borderline terrestrial worlds—just in the wrong place or state or proportions. The crystals provide the energy and guidance for the process. Depending on how much change is needed, five to fifty years later you've got a new world ready for the first colony ship."

In an empty galaxy, the Alliance could have carried on its missionary expansion until it ran out of will or worlds. But in time, the colonization efforts encroached on space occupied by the races Bhodi had seen depicted during Li-hon's presentation. Those races were then loosely organized under the rule of a dynastic clan. The world, the warlord, and their collective enemy were all named after the constellation they were found in: Arr, the vandal.

As a group, the Arrians viewed oxygen-breathers as little better than vermin and insisted they keep their distance. The Alliance decided that any creatures that rejected the truth of Photon and stood in the way of its spread where wholly evil and therefore not really alive at all.

There was as little chance for accommodation as for a compromise between flame and ether. War began with an Arrian attack on a crystal-siting team and had continued unabated for the better part of two hundred years.

"For all the fighting there's been, strategically it's been a stalemate until recently," Parcival noted. "The Arrians have learned how to reprogram the crystals so that they modify the planet's atmosphere to make it even more inhospitable to us. So where they used to just destroy the crystals, they now try to capture them and use them to deny us the worlds."

"Can't you just go in, shut the crystal down, fix the programming, and fire it up again?"

Parcival shook his head. "You remember how that warrior fired his phaser into the crystal to set it off? The phaser bolt triggers the microfusion capsule that drives the primary reaction. There's no shutting it off, and by the time it's exhausted the whole chemical momentum of the atmosphere has been changed.''

"But you can change it back."

"Usually—but changing it back takes just as long. And you still don't have things the way you want them. Add it all together and you see they can keep us off a world for a hundred years with one reprogrammed crystal," Parcival said. "But that's not all. The really scary prospect is of them bringing one to Earth or Foppo or Nivia and destroying the ecosystem."

"So that's what the war is really about—not the final battle between good and evil."

"No. Territory and theopolitics and biological racism."

"It makes a lot more sense the way you tell it. I feel a lot better."

"Yeah, well, you haven't heard the kicker yet."

"The kicker?"

Parcival looked down at his feet and frowned. "I wasn't going to tell you this, at least not yet. But I guess you've got a right to know going in. There is one big mystery I haven't been able to lay a glove on."

"What's that?"

"I don't know who the Ylem are."

"What!?"

"There are seven different species in the Alliance. I've been able to rule out two of them. But I don't know which of the others is the Ylem." He hesitated. "If any of them are."

"One of them has to be."

"That's what I thought. Then I started trying to find out who built the First Guardian—who makes the crystals— who designed our ships—and discovered that everybody thinks it's someone else. Ask Li-hon where the crystals come from and you get an answer something like 'The First Guardian provides.' "

"You mean that the Ylem might be hiding somewhere and letting you fight their battles?"

"Sometimes I think so." He shrugged. "Anyway. I guess the point for you is that you can't take everything you hear from the Alliance leadership at face value. But you can't go around challenging it, either."

"So is Earth really in danger? Or is that part of the fiction?"

"No," Parcival said somberly. "That's real. Look, I don't know what your habits are, but I'm ready to sack out. Do you mind?"

"What time is it? My watch is still in my locker at the Center."

"Midnight your time—the twenty-eighth division in ship time."

"Geez. I didn't realize," Bhodi Li said, standing up. "Except I don't know how well I'm going to sleep."

Parcival slipped past Bhodi in the narrow aisle and flung himself lengthwise on the cot. "These are more comfortable than they look."

"I meant because of everything there is to think about."

"Don't think too much—you'll hurt yourself." It was said teasingly, with a hint of a smile and a twinkle in the eye.

"I'll be careful," Bhodi Li said. He turned away as though to leave, but stopped at the door and looked back. "I can't help wondering about you—how you got here. Were you drafted, too? Nothing personal, but I've never seen anyone your age hold their own in the arena."

"I wasn't drafted, exactly. I volunteered."

"Volunteered! How?"

Parcival twisted onto his side and propped his head on one hand. "Truth is, I was always more interested in how the Photon Centers worked than the game itself—the sensors, the radios, the infrared guns, the computers. I poked around after hours and discovered a little too much. The First Guardian decided that I couldn't be let go and sent a ship to pick me up.''

''When was this?''

''Almost a year ago.''

''How often do you get back? I mean down to the surface.''

''I never do.''

''But your family—''

''There's nobody there to miss me,'' Parcival said, sounding like a ten-year-old for the first time since Bhodi had met him. ''This is the only home I've got. Look, I don't want to talk any more. I'm tired. Lights off,'' he added, and the room darkened.

''Sorry. G'night, Parcival. And thanks—for being straight with me.''

''You owe me one,'' Parcival said, settling back on the cot.

''Fair enough.'' Bhodi slapped the touchplate and watched the doorway magically appear.

''Hey—Bhodi,'' the youth suddenly called after him.

''What?''

''You play baseball?''

''Sure.''

Parcival nodded absently, staring at the ceiling. ''Think I'll ask them to pick up a glove for you the next time a ship stops at Earth. We can play catch anyway, right?''

''If I stay,'' Bhodi cautioned.

''That's what I meant. If you stay.'' But the hint of disappointment in Parcival's voice said that he had already begun to count on Bhodi's company.

What the hell am I going to do? Bhodi wondered as he returned to his quarters. *I'm a dozen light-years from home* with a lizard-priest that wants to convert me and a boy genius that wants me to be his big brother, on my way to boot camp for a star army. I don't want to fight for the First Guardian of Photon. I only came along for the ride—a sightseeing tour of the galaxy. But the more I see and learn, the harder it is to think about going back and forgetting it all.

And tomorrow we'll be there—wherever there is. What am *I* going to do?

CHAPTER 7

Bhodi Li stood on the bridge of the *Fraanic* and stared with wonder at the spectacle laid out before him on the windows of the scoutship. No recording this time, the great space station called Intellistar hung like a glittering toy in space, high above the fleecy yellow-tinged clouds of a golden world.

At any given time Bhodi could see at least a half-dozen other spacecraft moving against the dramatic backdrop formed by steady-shining stars, a great white moon, and the system's brilliant blue-white sun.

"This is like going into O'Hare or L.A.X.," Bhodi said to Parcival, who was standing nearby.

"It's always busy," Parcival agreed. "This is the nerve center for the whole Photon Force. The First Guardian is here, as much as she can be said to be anywhere. Most of our training facilities are in this system."

"In other words, this is home."

"For me, anyway," Parcival said.

As they orbited Intellistar awaiting their landing confirmation, the analogy to a metallic flower persisted in Bhodi's mind. The central core, hexagonal in shape, was surrounded by a halo of six "petals"—every other one drooping as though wilted. Above each of the drooping petals was a row of hanger bays. The smaller craft buzzing back and forth seemed like bees coming to prospect for pollen.

When they finally were cleared to approach, *Fraanic* herself took over and began a fully-automated hands-off docking. But Li-hon nevertheless stood by at the controls as insurance against a system failure.

"It's just occurred to me," Bhodi said as the silver skin of the space station eclipsed more and more of the sky. "Why do you even have ships? Why not use the spacetime transporter all the time?"

"Two reasons," Li-hon said. "One is energy. The other is design."

"Design?"

"The transporter needs a terminal at both ends," Parcival added. "We can't just plop people down wherever we like—or snatch them up, for that matter. That's why we had to take you right from the Photon Center."

"The goals. You've got them rigged up for the transporter."

Parcival bobbed his head in agreement. "Any good player ends up there eventually. But the other probe is more serious. It took a tremendous amount of energy to push this ship from Earth to here with the fractional drive—but it would have taken about three times as much energy to throw it the same distance."

"So it has a limited range."

"The operational limit is five milliparsecs, or about one trillion miles," Parcival said. "But just between you and me—when you're looking at more than a hundred million miles or so, if you have a choice between flying and being thrown, fly."

"And when you don't have a choice?"

"Knock on wood," Parcival said cheerily. "If you can find any."

Li-hon grinned, a disturbing sight. "Now you know why he carries a baseball bat along."

When they disembarked, they were greeted by a floating, green-glowing mote and a disembodied voice that said, "Welcome to Intellistar, Bhodi Li. If you will follow the Guide, the next stage in your challenge will begin."

"The Guide?"

Parcival gestured at the light. "The firefly. It'll show you where you need to go."

"You're not coming?"

"We can't help you with what's to come, Bhodi Li," said Li-hon.

"And what's that?"

The floating fire started down the corridor to the right. "Please follow the Guide, Bhodi Li," the voice said. It was female in character, even maternal. "Your questions will be answered at the proper time."

"Go on," Parcival urged. "And good luck."

"Thanks," Bhodi said, his voice reflecting the ambivalence he felt, and started in pursuit of the Guide. He glanced back once to find Li-hon and Parcival watching him with concerned looks as though seeing off a friend on a different journey.

What have I gotten myself into? he wondered as he followed the Guide around a corner. *Biology class is looking better and better all the time—*

The Guide led Bhodi through several hundred feet of corridors before bringing him to a small outfitting room. Inside, a black mesh bodysuit was neatly laid out on a white counter like a headless corpse.

"What you see before you is a personal body screen," the voice of the guide said. "Please get dressed."

"What for?"

"The body screen absorbs and redistributes the energy of a phaser hit. It is being provided so that you will not be encumbered by armor your body is unaccustomed to bearing."

"No—I meant why am I getting dressed? What's this about?"

"To continue your challenge, you must demonstrate your abilities in a combat audition. Did Sergeant Nar-lex-ko-li-hon not inform you?"

Bhodi Li fingered the material of the screen. Though it looked like it was woven of black wire, the mesh was as supple as jersey. "He told me. Does this go over my clothes?"

"Yes, Bhodi Li."

The body screen went on as though it had been custom-fit for him, body-hugging but nowhere binding or restricting. Sleeve-straps that caught in the crook of his thumb like a half-glove and foot-straps like those found on baseball pants made sure that his arms and legs were fully covered. Magical little closures brought the fabric up to a high collar.

As he fastened the last closure at the neck, there was a rustling sound behind him. He turned and found the counter arrayed with equipment that looked at first glance like a normal Photon Warrior's kit.

A second glance told Bhodi it was not. The chest sensor unit was more finely detailed, its receptor lenses faceted like jewels. The power belt weighed no more than half of what he expected, as though the batteries had been removed from the contoured boxes that rode on each hip. Unlike the helmet he had left in his cabin on *Fraanic,* this one had a low-riding neck skirt and wraparound face screen.

But it was the phaser pistol that sealed his understanding that this was a different game. It had greater heft, a different balance, but most of all a certain wicked look that

said that it could really do what those he had held before
could only pretend to.

"Please continue dressing," the Guide reminded.

"Sorry." As Bhodi strapped the power belt in place, his
apprehension started to fade, displaced by a growing anticipation. He wondered if the training arena would be laid
out the same as in his home center. *If this is a real phaser,
my opponent must be a hologram—or a robot—God, it'll
be like walking into a video game—*

"Ready," he said, slipping the helmet down over his
head and drawing the chin strap tight.

To Bhodi's right, the wall irised into a doorway. "Pro-
ceed, Bhodi Li."

Bhodi stepped through the opening. The room was tiny,
empty, blank-walled, and with no apparent exit. "What
now?" he asked.

As though in answer, the room came alive with electric
blue light, dancing on the surface of the walls, encasing
Bhodi Li in a halo of energy.

Transporter! Bhodi thought. *On the road again—*

When the transporter cocoon dissipated, Bhodi Li found
himself standing alone on a desolate plain littered with
spikelike outcrops of reddish rock. The landscape was in
twilight, yet the sun hung near the zenith, a blue-white
ghost slipping behind a high overcast of yellow clouds.
The ground underfoot was hard and unyielding under a
thin blanket of gray-black sand. A light wind blew across
the emptiness.

*No, not here—this isn't fair. I've never seen this place
before. How can I show what I can do—*

"Test your weapon, Bhodi Li." It was the voice of the
Guide, sounding inside his helmet.

Bhodi raised the phaser pistol experimentally and drew a
bead on the face of the nearest boulder. When he squeezed

the trigger, a pencil-thin red beam of light leapt from the barrel, and a shower of rock chips exploded from the spot that had been his target. But he had no time to marvel at the power that had been handed to him.

"Challenger Bhodi Li, prepare to do battle."

"Against what?"

There was no answer. It did not take long for Bhodi Li to begin to feel unnecessarily exposed standing alone on the flats. There was cover all around—cover that he should not cede to his opponent.

But as he broke into a trot in the direction of the nearest outcrop, a red flicker played across his facemask and slashed diagonally across his shoulder. He nearly screamed in shock and pain. It was as though his skin were being seared in a bath of liquid fire.

Instinctively, Bhodi turned his forward momentum into a diving forward roll that removed him from his adversary's gunsights. Scrambling into the protective shadow of a rock wall, he caught a glimpse of a wide-hipped thick-legged figure in tan fatigues. Then rock chips showered down on Bhodi as a phaser bolt struck inches above his head, and he ducked back out of sight.

Not human. Not Qeth. Another of the species Li-hon told me about. Looks slow—I should be able to outquick him, if not his phaser fire. The thought reminded Bhodi of the terrible pain that had inexplicably vanished. He looked down at his shoulder and saw to his surprise that the body screen was intact, his clothing and the skin beneath it apparently undamaged. The only evidence of the combat's opening exchange was a fine coating of dust on the mesh— dust from the surface of an alien world.

So the screen protects me from harm—but not from hurting, Bhodi thought as he scanned what he could see of the landscape for the threat of movement and the promise of better shelter. *If I were my opponent—*

Just as Bhodi was realizing with belated alarm that he'd been motionless too long, from behind he heard the sound of something hard sliding and grating on bare rock. His heart pounding, he scrambled halfway around the boulder in the opposite direction. He crouched there for a moment, then took off toward a cluster of cigarlike pinnacles and the jumble of rock at their base.

As he ran, he scanned the rockfall ahead for the best hiding place. Then he saw a flicker of red light play on the rock beyond him, and suddenly his back was tingling with anticipation of the shot to come. Bhodi went into a feet-first dive, as though he were sliding into third base. A half roll to the right put him on his belly, looking back the way he had come. He gripped his pistol in both hands as he drew a bead on the figure standing where he had crouched just moments before.

The squeezing of the trigger was reflex, or he would never have completed the act. This was a new enemy, tall and imposing, with a face like a mask and a body clad in articulated silver and black armor, carrying a long staff such as a wizard might own. The very sight of the wizard-warrior called all of Bhodi's self-confidence into question.

Bhodi's shot was on target, but pitiably ineffective. The beam of energy reflected harmlessly off the polished surface of the creature's breastplate and up toward the sun. Bhodi did not wait to try again. As the creature began to point the end of the staff in Bhodi's direction, fear drove him to his feet and toward the rockfall.

But this time, the wizard's aim was good. Pain exploded in the middle of Bhodi's back, dropping him to his knees. He crawled the last few feet to shelter in agony, the speakers in his helmet crackling with static from the overload of energy his body screen was laboring to dispose of.

Bhodi dove over the crumbling edge of a table-flat sheet of rock that had sheared off the tallest of the pinnacles, and the pain and heat began to ebb. He lay on the hard ground panting and wondering how many opponents he would have to face before the audition was over. He already felt hounded and harried, a new and unpleasant sensation.

Everything he had done so far had been defensive, he realized. He had surrendered the initiative to his opponents. *They act, I react. But that's not the way I fight. And if I keep it up, they're going to hunt me down for sure—*

Twisting around, Bhodi popped up and got off a shot that caught the wizard, who was advancing across the sandy plain toward him, full in the face. Momentarily blinded by the overload of the sensors in his mask, the wizard halted his advance and turned his head away.

Bhodi did not wait to see what happened next. Crouching, he scurried deeper into the rockfall. Through a fissure between two great boulders, he caught a glimpse of the stocky thick-legged alien circling around to the rear of the rockfall. It was more than a hundred yards away, but Bhodi paused long enough in the fissure to squeeze off a quick shot that he was sure would not betray his hiding place.

The shot missed, and an instant later the alien's answering fire showered Bhodi with rock fragments. Ducking back, Bhodi kept moving. *Nothing that big should be able to react that fast*, he complained silently. *Who am I fighting?* On either side of him, the walls of rock climbed higher. As they did, he scanned for a good place to climb to a higher vantage.

That was what saved Bhodi from an ugly surprise. As he rounded a corner into a small natural courtyard, he glimpsed a figure atop one of the rock walls—a cocoa-skinned woman, a girl rather, her shock of black hair banded by knotted red scarf, her left arm drawn back in the act of throwing. He ducked to his right, and a spinning metal disk whistled past and imbedded itself in the rock behind him like a knife in butter.

By the time the second disk was on its way, Bhodi was ready with his pistol. With a sweeping shot that was more luck than skill, he vaporized the disk in midair before it could reach him. The thrower was another matter; she bounded nimbly away as his phaser cut off suddenly, a green LED below the rear sight changing to red.

Momentarily disarmed, Bhodi retreated the way he had come, only to come face-to-face with the wizard, standing like a living barricade a dozen steps ahead in the narrow passageway.

"You die here," it said.

But that pronouncement, brief as it was, gave Bhodi his opportunity for escape. Ducking his head, Bhodi reversed direction again and ran at his best flat-out scamper through the little courtyard and out its other exit.

Suddenly he found himself out of the rockfall, standing unprotected in the open. Thirty feet away was the stocky alien, and Bhodi's appearance there seemed to have surprised him. There was a moment of hesitation on both sides, then Bhodi brought his pistol whipping up to eye level.

The LED was green again, but before he could fire, a blast from the alien's gun caught Bhodi's chest unit squarely. The light on his pistol went out entirely as a shower of sparks exploded from Bhodi's midsection.

Bhodi stared disbelievingly at his conqueror. Beneath the broad-rimmed helmet, which looked like nothing so much as a bush hat with a wraparound visor, were two widely-set yellow eyes in a forest of fine featherlike down. The stout legs on which it stood terminated in fan-shaped flippers; the creature's long-fingered hands looked as though they, too, might have been webbed before surgery rendered them more useful.

Slowly Bhodi lowered his pistol to his side. "You win," he said simply.

At that, the girl reappeared, dropping lightly onto her feet from the rock above. "Of course," she said arrogantly. "Any one of us could have beaten you."

"Just as I could have defeated any one of you," another voice intruded. Bhodi spun around to see the metal-man wizard emerge from among the rocks.

"You're a shameless braggart, Lord Baethan," the alien rejoined.

The wizard bowed slightly from the waist. "As it is said on the homeworld of the candidate, if you can make good on your claims, it's not bragging."

The girl looked at Bhodi with disdain. "Which proves that his world has neither wisdom nor warriors to contribute."

Bhodi said nothing. Moments later, a circular area on the face of a nearby rock began to pulse with blue light. As the transporter cocoon formed around him, Bhodi thought that at least he no longer had any decisions to make. He had failed his test of combat, and soon he would be going home.

CHAPTER 8

Stars. The first thing that Bhodi Li saw was thousands of stars. Three walls of the vast chamber to which he'd been brought were transparent, nine great windows offering a U-shaped panorama two stories high. The windows were tilted inward toward the twenty-foot-diameter hexagonal skylight, through which Bhodi could see the starless disk that was the nighttime face of the planet he still did not know the name of.

The chamber was like the great hall of a spacegoing castle, complete with a raised dias at one end that could easily have supported a throne for a king—or queen—of the stars. And surrounding Bhodi was the strangest retinue any monarch could have.

They were all there: Li-hon, Parcival, and his three opponents from the combat audition. All weapons were holstered; they stood and watched him silently, sizing him up, waiting for something.

He realized for the first time that they all wore variations of the Photon chest sensor and power belt. The girl's sensor pack was black and tapered, the wizard's integral with his chest armor, but nevertheless it provided some unity to contrast their wildly different physiques and combat gear.

He glanced down at the destroyed unit still dangling from his own neck. It was silly to keep wearing it. He tugged at the straps and let the unit slip to the floor.

"Welcome to the Sanctum, Bhodi Li," a voice said. It was a voice that was new and familiar at the same time. "And welcome back, Guardians of the Light."

As one, the others turned toward the dias. When Bhodi looked in that direction, he saw the figure of an older woman suspended in midair over the dias. Her hair respectably short, her face marked with smile lines. She looked maternal, even grandmotherly. That thought was enough to allow him to place the voice. It was the voice of the glowing Guide.

"I am the First Guardian for the Alliance of Light," she said. "On me has fallen the honor and duty of directing the warriors of the ninety worlds against the forces of evil and darkness that threaten us."

As she poke, Bhodi realized that, despite the detail and realism, the image was a projection. Whether the woman herself was real, safely secreted in some unknown location, he could not tell. The warriors treated the image as though she were both real and deserving of respect. That was his only clue.

"Bhodi Li, it is time for you to meet those who opposed you in your test on the surface of the world we call Rejia," the First Guardian continued. "I am grateful for their service, as I am grateful for the service of all who have answered the call.

"Lord Baethan of Celtar."

The wizard took one step forward, his face wearing the same cold and haughty expression it had during combat. But Bhodi realized belatedly that it was no mask. For there was no warrior under the armor; the armor *was* the warrior. Lord Baethan was a machine—perhaps a robot, perhaps a cyborg. Either way, he was both the most fascinating and the most imposing figure in the room.

"Tivia of the Empire of Women."

She raised her left arm in a closed-fist salute. Bhodi had taken her for human, but he saw now that she was not. Under her thigh armor, cross-laced leggings and arm wrap, and Photon combat gear, she wore a net body stocking that resembled his body screen. But her net extended up over her mouth and nose, as though she could not breath the air the others did without filtering.

"Ferthewillihan Pike of the Foppo Intersystem Union."

The alien winked in Bhodi Li's direction. It was still wearing its helmet, and Bhodi Li wondered if the wrap-around visor was Pike's version of Tivia's filter net, modifying in some way the atmosphere that it was breathing. It seemed unlikely that species as different as the Fops, the Qeth, and Homo sapiens all grew up on worlds with identical oxygen-nitrogen atmospheres.

"And my warriors Parcival of Earth and Nar-lex-ko-li-hon of Qeth, who brought you into our company."

"Why are you dragging this out?" Bhodi asked impatiently. "Just tell me when I'm going home."

"Is that your choice?" Li-hon asked, surprised.

"How dense do you think I am? I flunked my audition," Bhodi said. "I don't need to wait for a report card to know that."

"Why do you think you failed, Bhodi Li?" asked the First Guardian.

"They had me on the run the whole time. The one shot I laid on target didn't so much as blister the paint on Baethan's armor. I never even scored a hit on the other two. Meanwhile they killed me about three times by my count. No, I flunked all right. Not that I ever had a chance. It wasn't a fair test."

"How was it not fair?" asked Lord Baethan. "It was you that had the screen and the full-force phaser. We were the ones at risk."

"Fair?" Bhodi said hotly. "Three against one, with you already hidden in the arena when I get there?" He turned to Li-hon. "I had no chance to scout the terrain, no chance to match one-on-one with any of them, no chance period. What's the point of a test nobody can pass?"

"What a fool and a child you are," Tivia said. "Do you think that the Arrians fight 'fair'? Do you expect them to give you a map of the battle zone and queue up to fight you one at a time—"

"Enough," the First Guardian said, and Tivia fell silent. "Bhodi Li. You are accustomed to victory. By the standards of the arena, you are an accomplished fighter. But by the standards of the Photon Force, you are a promising novice, nothing more. You were not expected to win."

"They why—"

"Be quiet and listen. As volunteers in a combat audition, your opponents had the option of fighting with screens. They chose not to, because to be defeated by you would have brought such great shame that death would be preferable. This is how vast the difference in your skills now is. I have little doubt that Tivia is annoyed that she failed to deliver a potentially killing blow against you."

Tivia scowled, confirming the First Guardian's supposition.

"All you're doing is telling me that it was even more unfair than I thought," Bhodi said. "What was the point? What could you learn?"

"It was not a test of skill," Li-hon said. "It was a test of heart. And you passed."

"I ran."

"You did not panic. You did not freeze. You fought as best you could with the skills and tools available to you."

Bhodi stared at Li-hon, then looked past him to the figure of the First Guardian. "I can stay?"

"If that is your choice," the First Guardian said. "Bhodi Li, you have earned on merit the right to challenge for a place among the Guardians of Light. Once you have been asked, and once you have refused. Now I ask you a second time: Will you give up your challenge?"

Bhodi looked slowly around him at the circle of warriors. Parcival's eyes were hopeful but his expression solemn. Behind her filter net, Tivia's mouth was twisted in disdain or lingering displeasure—Bhodi could not say which. Pike smiled a friendly smile. Lord Baethan and Li-hon were ciphers, their faces offering no clues to their emotions.

It doesn't get any better than this, Bhodi thought. *If I go back, it's to biology class and cutting the lawn and poring through college catalogs. Chances like this don't come up back there—*

Then he shifted slightly, and his foot brushed against the burned-out chest pack lying on the floor. One glance down at its blackened and melted face was enough to put a different shading on his thoughts. He remembered the pain and the hounded feeling and wondered how much worse the moment would have been if he had not known it was a test, an exercise, a game.

I died three times on Rejia. How long would it be before I died for real, and there's no one to send back to rescue my family and friends from the phantom timeline—

He looked around the circle again, and this time he saw five Photon Warriors, each quietly confident of his or her superiority, secure in the knowledge that they could defeat him. On Earth, Bhodi had climbed to the top of the ladder—only to catch the bottom rung of the next.

This isn't final, after all, he thought. *I get one more*

chance to refuse. Let's play it out. I want to see how far up the ladder I can go.

"No," Bhodi said, loudly and clearly. "I won't give up my challenge."

"Very well, Bhodi Li," said the First Guardian as her image began to fade. "Let your training begin."

Tivia and Lord Baethan took the withdrawal of the First Guardian as their cue to leave the Sanctum. They did so without a word to Bhodi or any of the others, as though they disapproved of what had happened there.

In that same long moment, Parcival was breaking into an easy grin and throwing himself into a hug with Pike, though his arms barely reached halfway around the rotund alien.

Pike grinned and hugged back. "Just returned from a mission," he explained, noting Bhodi's curiosity. "Don't mind the others. Lord Baethan's never voted in favor of a candidate yet, and Tivia would never vote in favor of a male—especially one she failed to put in his place."

Pike released Parcival, who took a step back. As he did, a flashing movement of the alien's right hand knocked the youth's cap off his head, then caught it in midair and returned it to where it had been. Parcival laughed and reached under the cap to retrieve a small sharp-edged rock with blue and blue-green veining.

"Kyranilite?"

"From Maldea," Pike said. "That was one you were missing, wasn't it?"

"Thanks, Uncle Pike."

Bhodi's ears perked up with curiosity at Parcival's chosen form of address, but he said nothing about it. "It was a committee decision, then? Democracy in the ranks?"

"A platoon one," Li-hon said. "We will all have to fight alongside you, after all."

"And they don't much want to. Who did vote for me, then?"

"Look around you," Li-hon said.

"I did," Parcival added.

"So did I," Pike said cheerily. "But then, I've never voted against a candidate I had the pleasure of frying. I always like to give them another chance to return the favor."

"What Pike really enjoys is having a chance to make side bets with the station staff on who makes it through training and what breaks them if they don't," Li-hon interjected. "Did you have any action on the audition?"

"A little."

"How'd you come out?"

"The heavy money was on Lord Baethan to drop Bhodi," Pike said, beaming. "I did very nicely."

Li-hon shook his head. "Bhodi, tell me when you're ready to move into your quarters and I'll call a Guide. You'll be in the trainee barracks, called Section Yellow."

"No need for a Guide," Parcival said. "I'll take him down."

"Are you sure? I thought you'd want to get back to your lab as soon as you could."

"It's no problem."

A few minutes later they excused themselves and started down a long sloping corridor toward the central core of the station.

"What did you see?" Parcival asked eagerly when they were alone.

"What do you mean?"

"When you looked at the First Guardian. Describe her to me."

"Uh—a woman, middle-aged, I guess. Kind of plain and elegant looking at the same time. I thought she looked like somebody's mother."

"What color?"

"Huh?"

"Her skin," Parcival said impatiently. "What color was it?"

"Why, white—"

"Good—good! Did she look like *your* mother?"

"Um—a little bit. I guess. Same build—tall and slender. Maybe my mother plus ten years. She didn't sound like her, though."

"Oh," Parcival said, frowning disappointedly.

"I don't get it. Isn't that what you see?"

The boy shook his head. "No. I see a round-faced black woman, about thirty pounds overweight, twenty-eight or so. Li-hon sees a Qeth clutch keeper—six foot of mean mama lizard. Tivia sees a woman she describes as the Nivian High Priestess."

"Everybody see something different?"

"Yeah. I thought I had it figured out, but I guess I don't."

"What did you mean?"

"I was hoping that you would see your own mother. Then I would know that the woman I was seeing is mine."

Bhodi stopped short and stared. "You don't know what your mother looks like?"

Parcival shook his head. "Or her name, or why she didn't want to keep me."

He said it casually, but Bhodi knew there had to be pain somewhere inside, an irreducible knot of agony that could not be intellectualized away. Yet for all his empathy, Bhodi could find nothing but the mawkish and obvious to say. "You're an orphan?"

"I don't like that word," Parcival said, starting down the corridor once more. "I'm an abandoned child. As far as I know, I never lived with my mother or any of her family. She went out the front door of the hospital, and I went out the back.

"Do you know, I once tried to calculate the odds that I had already crossed paths with her and not known it. I was always looking at black women of the right age, trying to see myself in their faces. I might have been in the same shopping mall with her, or in the same subway."

Still he did not sound bitter, and Bhodi was puzzled. "Why bother? She didn't give you anything."

"She gave me life," Parcival said pointedly. "Look, I know it's hard to understand, but I don't hate her, whoever she is. I'm glad she took it as far as she did. I'm willing to believe it was as far as she could." He stopped abruptly and reached for a touchplate. "We're here."

The door irised open, but Bhodi made no move to enter. "So why was it important to know what she looked like?"

Parcival folded is arms over his chest as though he were hugging himself. His eyes were cast downward in the direction of Bhodi's feet. "I don't know. It just is. She gave me up. I guess I'd like to know why."

"You came out of it pretty well, though. Look at you. Smarter than anything, and a good enough fighter to become a Guardian."

Parcival looked up and tried to smile. "Thanks. I guess I did come out okay. But you know, I figured out a couple of months ago—one of the reasons is I'm always trying to prove that I would have been worth keeping."

CHAPTER 9

"Let your training begin," the First Guardian had said. But it proved not to be as simple as that.

He was taken first to the staff adjutant, who conducted a brief station orientation, assigned Bhodi a sleeping room, and then gave him a credit chip and identification band. The credit chip was a six-sided phenolic coin with which Bhodi could tap his training stipend for expenses above and beyond room and board. The ID band was an oval bracelet of copper-colored metal, which filled the vacancy if not the void left by the twelve-function watch resting uselessly in a locker on Earth.

The adjutant explained that the band was the "key" which opened doors on Intellistar. Unlike on board *Fraanic*, access to many parts of Intellistar were controlled by status and security clearances. Bhodi discovered he was even required to touch a scanner when moving from one color-coded section of the station to another.

When his business there was finished, the staff adjutant sent Bhodi on to the medical section for his physical evaluation. Bhodi spent more than twenty hours over the next three days being subjected to a battery of tests by a gracile, slender-limbed alien doctor named Irini'g't. According to the alien, Bhodi's entire training regiment would be customized according to what the examination revealed.

At Irini'g't's direction, Bhodi ran, jumped, swam, strained with weights until his muscles turned to rubber. He lay on tables while exotic machines passed over his body, probing and scanning. He sat in a pitch-black room and listened for whispering voices lost in a roar like ocean surf.

"The object is not to make you perfect," Irini'g't explained. "No individual can embody all of its species' capabilities, and no species is without its inbred deficiencies. Our goal is to identify the unrealized potential in your body and decide how best to push you in the direction of your own limits."

"Has everyone gone through this?"

"Each according to his needs. There was little we could do for Nar-lex-ko-li-hon that his experience in the Qeth's War of Bloody Tears hadn't already seen to. While Lord Baethan is always undergoing modifications—though such matters are handled by his peers on Celtar, and not here on Intellistar."

"What is Lord Baethan, exactly?"

"Difficult," Irini'g't said shortly. "I *am* rather proud of the work we did with Ferthewillihan Pike. There were many who thought that it would be impossible to make a Guardian out of a Fop. Though there are those who will say they wish I hadn't succeeded," he added. "Keep your eye on your money when Pike's around."

"Are you saying he's a thief?"

"I prefer not to be so legalistic. Let it be understood that Pike has fast hands."

"And sticky fingers?"

"Not usually. He has other ways of separating you from your possessions. And he seems to consider it a point of honor to take every trainee at least once before they wash out," said Irini'g't.

"Thanks for the warning."

"I warn everyone. It rarely does any good. Enough gossip, Bhodi Li. Turn on your back, please—"

When the medical section was finally finished with him, the next stop on Bhodi Li's itinerary was the outfitter. There he selected three sets of what the outfitter called "customaries"—everyday clothes whose designs were borrowed from homeworld fashions but realized the local materials. Bhodi ended up with jeans of a tough flexible fabric that he was sure would neither fade nor fringe satisfactorily; his pullover shirts looked like cotton but shed water like a London Fog raincoat.

But the clothing that mattered most was that which he would wear in combat. To get it he had to pay a visit to the Alliance armorer, a Fop whose downy, pale-yellow facial covering ruffled when he shook his head.

"Human, eh?" he said, studying Bhodi with one arm crossed over his chest and the other propping up his chin. "Well, it's head-to-toe protection for you. Never have seen a species with thinner skin or more pain receptors. It's like packaging an egg to get you ready for battle."

The bodysuit the armorer produced five minutes later was form-fitting without being the least restrictive. It moved freely in any direction Bhodi could, thanks to several panels of accordionlike pleats in critical areas.

Over his feet went comfortable square-toed boots that rose halfway up his calf. The gloves had long thick cuffs and reinforced panels on the back of the hand, but the fingers were thin enough that he swore he could feel a hair lying on a tabletop, and maybe even pick it up. A teardrop-bubble helmet with a gray smoke tint completed the suit.

"On an Oh-two world you can use a pot helmet instead of the bubble," the armorer said, stepping back like a fussy tailor to study his handiwork. "The evaluation report says we're going to bulk you up a little bit, so when any of this starts to get uncomfortable you come back.''

''It all feels a little uncomfortable right now.''

''It's a new suit. Break-in period's about ten days. Where do you want armor?''

''I don't know,'' Bhodi said, surprised to be asked. ''What do you usually do?''

''Humans have too many vulnerable points to armor them all. If I did, you couldn't move to fight. And I've been ordered not to slow you down.'' The armorer drummed his fingers on the back of his head as he glanced from Bhodi to his data screen and back again. ''We'll want cuisses, anyway.''

''Huh?''

''Thigh shields. Holster on the right?''

''Uh—yes.''

Each piece was custom-molded in accord with Bhodi's measurements as he watched. The thigh shields protected the front, side, and back of each thigh, and were strapped in place with elastic bands that Bhodi hoped would keep the shields from ending up around his ankles when he ran.

The chest and back armor was made of dozens of small plates, like a turtle's shell, connected with more of the flexible material used for the straps. When it was in place, he tried drawing a deep breath. There was only the slightest pressure on his chest.

Small shoulder shields called cops came next, and then finally two boxy pieces of armor for his left arm, like smaller versions of the thigh shields. One strapped to his bicep, the other to his forearm, with an extension that protected the back of the hand and curled ninety degrees at the end to cup around his fingers.

''What's this for?'' Bhodi asked, flexing the arm experimentally.

''You have to see to shoot, don't you?''

"Usually helps."

"But if you stick your head up, people shoot at *you*. And even with a helmet, the head is vulnerable." Gripping an imaginary pistol in his right hand, the armorer crossed his left arm over the right at the wrist and sighted toward the far wall. "See? The left arm partly shields your head. You give them only half as much target. Your weapons instructor will show you more."

"If it's such a good idea, why doesn't anyone else wear them?"

"I told you before, Bhodi Li. Each to his best skills."

"What are mine?"

The Fop smiled. "When you know, you'll be ready to graduate. That's all, Bhodi Li. Report to the training supervisor at Yellow 14."

Bhodi tapped the pistol recess on the right thigh shield. "Don't I get something to fill this?"

The armor shook his head. "First you learn to fight without it."

The training supervisor was a Qeth named Haj-til-ko-van. His leathery skin was a lighter green than Li-hon's; later, Parcival told him that that meant he was several decades younger, as the skin darkened throughout a Qeth's life.

"The training division has no permanent instructors," Haj-til-ko-van explained. "Since you are challenging for a place with the Ninth Platoon under the command of Sergeant Nar-lex-ko-li-hon, whenever possible your instructor will be the sergeant himself or another member of that platoon."

Bhodi groaned at the prospect of suffering under the tutelage of Tivia or Lord Baethan. *They'll be hazing me for sure, since they didn't want me here at all.* "Why is that?'' Bhodi asked. "I'd think that their time would be too valuable for teaching. Or are things quiet now?''

"Hardly. The Arrian Alliance is pushing us harder now than at any time since the war began. No, the reason we do this is to let you become familiar with the men and women you hope to fight alongside, and for them to become familiar with you. The members of an effective combat team don't need to be friends, but they do need to know each other's abilities.''

"So we work together effectively. Yeah, that makes sense.''

"Plus there's no lag in bringing the lessons and experiences of the field to the training of new Guardians. And unlike an instructor who never has to fight, your platoon has a vested interest in seeing that you're trained properly.''

"I can see that. I guess I didn't realize that I was already spoken for, though.''

"Nothing will be given to you, Bhodi Li," Haj-til-ko-van warned. "You will earn a place on merit or be allowed to go home.''

"I understand.''

Haj-til-kov-van looked down at his scheduler. "I am your physical conditioning coach. We will begin your designed program immediately and continue it each afternoon. Tomorrow morning you will begin studying close-order fighting with Tivia as your instructor.''

Bhodi's spirits fell. *Why'd it have to be her first thing?* "Do I meet her here?''

"You do." Haj-til-ko-van pointed behind Bhodi at a doorplate. "You will find training clothes in the dressing room. I expect you in the arena in three minutes or less.''

Bhodi's eyes widened. "Yes, sir," he said reflexively, backpedaling in the direction Haj-til-ko-van had pointed. As he reached for the doorplate, he called across the room, "How many vacancies are there in the platoon, anyway?''

"One at present," Haj-til-ko-van said. "Li-hon lost his combat partner in a firefight on Frea 6 earlier this year."

"Combat partner?"

"Many missions do not require full platoon strength. The platoons are organized as three combat pairs."

And Li-hon wants me to fight alongside him—what do you know about that! "One last question. How long will my training take?"

Haj-til-ko-van teased his front teeth with the tip of his tongue before answering. "Only you can determine that, Bhodi Li—and you seemed determined to prolong it. Now dress! We have much work to do."

That night, Bhodi lay in his bunk exhausted but unable to sleep. His body was registering, a thousand complaints about the treatment it had received at Haj-til-ko-van's hands. He was not hurt, but he was hurting. He sneezed once, and the resultant pain nearly made him cry out.

There were three major goals to the physical conditioning program—more strength, more speed, and more agility. Haj-til-ko-van seemed to expect to get all three at once. Bhodi's workout plan contained fifty-seven different items from every exercise discipline—aerobic, yogic, isometric and more. Between them not a muscle in his body seemed to have escaped being stretched, stressed or strained.

On top of that, there was the humiliation of discovering that the stylish broken-seven symbol of the back of the training clothes was the equivalent of the practice-field redshirt—a proclamation that the wearer was too green to be subject to full contact. Bhodi hated the thought of facing Tivia in the morning wearing the brand. The moment he could graduate to clothes without it could not come too soon.

There had been a dozen other trainees of assorted biological heritage in the training arena (Bhodi would have called it a gym). Later Bhodi had seen several of the same faces in the dining hall, though he had been too tired to be convivial. All told, there seemed to be no more than twenty-five or thirty trainees on station, all quartered together in Yellow section within a three-minute walk of the training arena.

Could that possibly be all there are? Bhodi wondered. It was impossible to guess. What was the dropout rate? What level of casualties did the Force suffer? Probably both facts were classified. But it seemed likely that if this were the only training center, the entire Photon Force might number no more than five hundred warriors.

Five hundred warriors to fight a war that spanned thousands of light-years—

Staring up at the ceiling in the darkness, Bhodi realized that he missed Parcival. The youth had walked him through what could have been some very tough adjustments, helping him come to grips with the fantastic thing that had happened and the incredible place he found himself. Bhodi wished he could walk down the corridor right at that moment and invite himself in for some late-night conversation.

But this wasn't the *Fraanic*, and Parcival wasn't down the hall. In fact, Parcival and Pike were off-station already, having flown off on another mission within hours of the ceremony in the Sanctum. Bhodi was on his own. On his own, and alone with the thought that was keeping him awake:

I don't want to fail—

Bhodi was early, determined not to be found wanting on any count. Tivia was late, as though to say the whole business was an unwelcome responsibility. She walked past him without offering any greeting, a small drawstring bag dangling from one hand. He followed, and she led him to a private training room. The room was long and narrow. The end where they entered had padded walls and floor. The far wall was covered by concentric red squares, like a target.

"Ja-Nin is a discipline of the mind," she said, kneeling and beginning to empty the contents of the bag onto the padding before her. "Because you are a male, you can never learn the essence of Ja-Nin. I will try to teach you its weapons."

"What is this problem you have about men?"

She looked up at him coldly. "There are eight weapons in the Ja-Nin," she continued, ignoring his question. "The mind, the senses, the hands, the feet—these are with you always, and are known as the Greater Instruments. The arm knife, the throwing disk, the double club, the nonchuks—"

"What?"

She held up something that looked like a masochist's jump rope—a sturdy chain about three feet long with a hexagonal metal grip on either end.

"Oh—you *are* answering questions," Bhodi said. "How about answering my first one? Why can't a man master the Ja-Nin?"

"Because he is a male," she said dismissively. "These are the Lesser Instruments," she continued, taking in the weapons with a sweep of her hand. "Circumstance or a skilled opponent can deny you the Lesser Instruments, but nothing except your own weakness can deprive you of the Greater Instruments—"

The realization that Tivia had written him off in advance simply because of his gender infuriated Bhodi. "Wait," he said sharply. "We've got something to settle first."

"What is that?"

"The First Guardian said that you were annoyed that you didn't score on me during the audition. Was she right?"

"To miss such an easy target betrays a loss of Ja-Nin harmony."

Bhodi half smiled. "Sent you back to the practice range, eh?"

"The failure was not the fault of the arm, but the mind. I spent three hours in meditative exercise regaining form."

"I'll give you a chance to test the repair job," Bhodi said. "Let's you and I break the draw right now—Greater Instruments only." *Come on, Your Smugness,* he urged silently. *I've got two years of aikido that you've never seen, because I can't use it playing Photon. Give me a chance to surprise you.*

"The offer is not without its attractions," she said, her gaze piercing. "But if I hurt you, Haj-til-ko-van will curse my days for the next three cycles. We will begin your study of the Ja-Nin with—"

"It's this, isn't it?" he snapped, clawing at the pullover shirt with the offending ideogram. Whipping it over his head, he flung the shirt to the base of the nearest wall. "Now you don't have to hold back. Now I'm nobody special. Let's go."

She faced him with arms akimbo and slowly shook her head. "Put your shirt back on."

"Come on, what's it take?" Bhodi demanded, taking a step forward. "Or maybe you're worried I'll hurt you."

"You can't," she said bluntly.

His hands closed into fists. "Prove it."

Tivia sighed. "You asked why males fail to achieve Ja-Nin harmony. One reason is they don't know when not to fight," she said, dropping into a semi-crouch with her hands raised and open in front of her. "Come, then, and learn."

CHAPTER 10

True to her obligations as instructor, Tivia did not hurt Bhodi. But she handled him easily and humbled him thoroughly. None of his previous martial arts training was of any value whatsoever. Tivia was more agile, more versatile, but most surprisingly, more ferocious.

Each time she had him in a killing hold or took him down with a potentially fatal checked-force blow, she told him so—and seemed to take pleasure in doing so. Released, he would have a few seconds to try to gather his breath and confidence, and then she would be on the attack again.

There was not a moment during the whole encounter when he had the advantage, and there came at last a moment when he knew that however long they continued, he never would. When she saw that new humility in his eyes, she signaled the end of their duel and resumed the lesson without a word.

They worked together each morning for a week, taking up a new weapon in each session. Bhodi had never tried to learn so much so quickly. Tivia explained the theory behind each of the weapons, described the advantages and disadvantages of each, and demonstrated the technique required to use it correctly. Then she left him alone to practice, alone or with another trainee.

He was surprised at first by that behavior. Later he became annoyed. It seemed as though she were saying that she did not consider tutoring him a good use of her time. Not only did it deprive him of her experience, it eliminated any chance he had to chart his progress relative to her skills.

Even more curious was that when she returned at the end of the session to observe him, she offered no critique. His questions were answered with paraphrases of what she had already told him.

He knew that Ja-Nin was meant to promote self-reliance, but it seemed as though she were using that principle as a pretext for setting him up to fail. So he ignored his body's protests and worked far harder than he otherwise might have, including arranging extra practice sessions at night with other trainees.

On the last day of Tivia's tutelage, Bhodi got brave enough to ask a question that had nagged at him from the beginning—how it was that such skills were needed in a war being fought with spaceships and phaser weapons.

"All struggles are ultimately decided by the Greater Instruments," was her simple reply.

"A phaser at a hundred yards or a ship's battery at a thousand will decide it a long time before you can get close enough to wrap your nunchuks around your opponent's neck."

Rebuttal came not from Tivia, but from Haj-til-ko-van, who had entered silently behind them.

"Their ships have shields. Our ships have shields. Their warriors have body armor. Our warriors have armor and screens," the training supervisor said matter-of-factly. He bowed to Tivia. "Thank you for your efforts, *Daryama* Tivia. We will monitor the candidate's progress from now on."

She nodded silently, smoothly swept up her gear, and was gone.

"Bhodi Li," Haj said sternly when she was gone. "When all Lesser Instruments fail, a warrior lives or dies on his command of the Greater Instruments—first among them the mind. Remember that one truth, Bhodi Li, and you may live to outgrow your ignorance. A useful short-term goal would be to survive combat gunnery training, which you will begin tomorrow."

When Bhodi returned to his quarters after his workout that afternoon, he found a message waiting for him with the welcome news that Parcival and Pike were back on-station.

"Don't make plans for dinner," it said over Parcival's name. "I'll call when we escape from debriefing, and we'll do something."

The prospect was enough to drive much of the fatigue from Bhodi's limbs. He took the shower he had postponed at the arena, and the call came as he was toweling off. This time it was Pike.

"You ready?" the alien asked cheerfully. "I'm starving."

"I'm five minutes from ready."

"Excellent. Do you know how to find your way to Dock 16?"

"I haven't really done much exploring—" The truth was that, his exhausting schedule notwithstanding, it had never occurred to him that there might be reasons to leave Section Yellow, and that he might be free to do so.

"It's on Level 20 on Section Blue. Go out to the main corridor and come two sections sunwise around to rim. You know the sequence—like the spectrum. Red, orange, yellow, green, blue, violet. Then take a speedlift to 20. Got it?"

Pike had rattled off the instructions so quickly that

Bhodi wasn't at all sure that he did have it. But he gamely said yes, hung up, and got on with dressing. Three minutes later he was going out the door.

Bhodi saw Pike first. He was standing near the security gate for Dock 16, wearing what looked like a mad seamstress's version of a safari jacket. Pike's khaki bodysuit was festooned with more than twenty button-flap pockets of assorted sizes, from pairs of tiny ones on the half sleeves to a wide pouchlike pocket in the middle of Pike's belly.

But what caught Bhodi's eyes was a surprising splash of color. For the first time in Bhodi's experience, the Fop was bare-headed, revealing a scarlet crest from mid-forehead back over the top of his skull, like a feathery mohawk.

Pike was turned half away, caught up in animated conversation with the gate guard. Parcival was standing a few feet away, scanning the passing foot traffic.

"Yo!" Bhodi called, his hand shooting up.

Parcival's face brightened. "There you are. And you seem to have survived Tivia."

"Don't bring up ugly subjects," Bhodi said. "I'm glad you came back okay."

"It wasn't hard. There wasn't any fighting," Parcival said. "We got there too late."

"Oh. Sorry to hear that—I think. Where are we going?"

"Dirtside," Pike said, joining them.

"Am I allowed?"

"Sure—but don't be surprised they didn't tell you. The First Guardian's a prude."

"No, she's not. She's an ascetic," Parcival disagreed.

"The difference makes no difference. You still can't have any fun on Intellistar."

The opening was there; Bhodi took it without thinking. "Besides, too many people know you here."

Pike stared, then laughed heartily. "Haj-til-ko-van has been telling tales on me again, I see."

"No tales. Just warnings."

"Then I'll tell you the tales myself," Pike said cheerily, laying a long-fingered hand on Bhodi's shoulder and squeezing. "They're all lies, but entertaining ones. Come on, touch in and let's board, before the captain forgets how many favors he owes me and reels in the gangway."

The ship anchored on Dock 16 looked like something lifted from an aircraft engineer's dream-doodle pad, with a sleek aerodynamic hull and a superthin delta wing. Inside, the windowless cabin had two ranks of plushly carpeted and thickly padded pits in place of rows of seats. Each pit was large enough to hold one Fop or Qeth or a couple members of any other Alliance species.

"Not quite like riding the subway," Parcival said, noticing Bhodi's interest.

"Not quite. I guess seating is a problem in mixed company."

Parcival bobbed his head in agreement. "Even when all the species are upright and bipedal. This is the best solution anyone's come up with."

Several of the pits were already filled with passengers, and several of the passengers were clearly impatient with the delay. But as Pike ambled down the center aisle ahead of Bhodi and Parcival, he exchanged greetings with many of them and the irritation vanished from their faces and voices.

"Everybody seems to know Pike."

"And he loves it," Parcival said as they came to an unoccupied pit. "Here, you and I can take this one."

"I assume we're riding this thing because it's more efficient than the transporter," Bhodi said, following the youth into the pit at hand.

"That, and because we're not going to an official Alliance facility."

"How rough is the ride?" Bhodi asked, looking in vain for any sort of safety restraint.

"Barely 1.8 gees, and that down through the axis of the body if you're sitting up. But that's plenty to keep you planted. You won't end up on the ceiling—unless we crash, in which case it doesn't matter."

Bhodi looked dubious. "Where *are* we going, anyway?"

The ship lurched slightly as the dock grapples released it to space. "Dracona."

"What's it like?"

Parcival chuckled. "Like Uncle Pike says, you can have fun there."

If there was a reason for Dracona, it was the simple principle that people who live on the edge need to play on the edge to keep their sanity. That was as true of Qeth, Fop, Riknoid, and Ikthalarian as it was for humans; less true of Nivians, though that may have been a matter of taste rather than temperament.

The one real exception was the Celtans, who looked on Dracona as a proof of the weakness and imperfection of those who frequented it. Celtans were seen there only in the conduct of official errands, such as retrieving errant platoon-mates in danger of missing a muster. What, if anything, the Celtans themselves required in the way of relaxation was a continuing mystery.

Nothing about Dracona had the blessing of Alliance decision-makers, not even its existence. It had sprung up like a concrete and flexiform weed on the wind-favored eastern coast of Rejia's largest sea, an unofficial colony under the nose of the top colonization planners. But despite the city's ambiguous status, vanishingly little effort was made to keep station personnel and members of the

Force away, or even to make life difficult for the city managers.

Proof of that was easily found. Freight for the city trans-shipped through the station's docks; deep-space communications to and from Dracona were relayed through the station's communications center. True, all such services were paid for by the dirtsiders on a cost-plus-tax basis. But the fact that the First Guardian even allowed those transactions was taken by most as a tacit acknowledgment that there was a need for what Dracona provided—which was what all such communities have always provided: sex, food and recreation.

For the Fops and Qeth, who like Homo sapiens were blessed or cursed by year-round mating urges, there was companionship—both casual and professional. There were eateries of every description offering fare from every cuisine. Assorted intoxicants were available, though not much in demand among the Guardians. And those looking to be entertained could choose from the popular arts of seven cultures—though the selection was admittedly skewed toward the raucous, the bawdy and the exotic.

But most of all, what Dracona offered was games. Silly and serious, organized and informal, the city's inhabitants and its visitors loved games. Dracona offered a chance for the Guardians to exorcise their natural competitiveness without the penalty for defeat being death.

And because the Guardians set the tone for what was admired, not only on Intellistar but throughout the Alliance, Dracona's game offerings had grown far beyond a casual round of pockets in the back room or wrestling match in the street outside a bar. From quoits to q'arim, from banuja to bell-of-warning, Dracona was the place where champions came to prove themselves.

"Is this really the same planet my audition was held on?" Bhodi wondered aloud.

He had paused at the top of the disembarkment ramp to look out through the transparent walls at the bustling city. None of the buildings was taller than a few stories, but the whole coastline was splendid with flashing laser lights.

"Just like the Sahara is on the same planet with Tokyo and Mexico City," Parcival said.

"Stop gabbing," Pike said. "If I have to wait much longer to eat I'm going to start thinking about broadening my diet to include humans. Though you'd look awfully silly on the platter."

Nearly an hour passed before Bhodi fully understood Pike's macabre joke.

The first third of that time was spent in a taxi, an odd little vehicle that looked like a bathtub slung between two bicycles. Eateries offering Terran foods were a minority, and the one Pike had chosen was near the northern end of Dracona's Main Street "strip." The crush of vehicles and pedestrians made what should have been a five-minute taxi ride three times longer, leaving time for conversation.

"I'm surprised that any of the restaurants cater to humans. After all, how many of us are on-station?" Bhodi asked as they picked their way through traffic.

"There are 108 humans attached to Intellistar," Parcival said. "Sixty-nine males and thirty-nine females. There are another thirteen humans located at other facilities in the system."

Surprise registered on Bhodi's face. "That's about a hundred more than I'd have thought. Where've they been hiding? I haven't seen any other trainees from Earth."

"Most are general station staff," Parcival said. "You ordinarily wouldn't run into them."

"Most of them wouldn't want to run into you," Pike amended. "Nothing personal—a matter of pride. They're all culls, brought here as challengers and failed to make it for one reason or another.''

Bhodi twisted sideways to look at Pike. ''I didn't know staying was an option when you wash out.''

''There's more to an army than its warriors,'' Pike said with a shrug. ''If someone's got the right outlook and skills we can use, there's a place for them.''

''So how many of those hundred and whatever are Guardians?''

''One,'' Parcival said, reentering the discussion. ''And he'd appreciate it if you'd get your elbow out of his ribs.''

''Sorry,'' Bhodi said, settling back in his seat.

''Mmm, ribs—'' Pike murmured.

''There's no meat on me,'' Parcival demurred. ''Try Bhodi.''

''Now, just a minute—''

''Hop Zoid's Grill,'' the driver announced.

''Lucky Bhodi,'' Pike said, clambering out. ''Thanks, Clarence. I'll knock a five off your debt.''

''Order whatever you want,'' Pike urged when they were settled in their seats.

Of the half dozen Terran dishes offered, the best-sounding one was bar chicken. It came steam-cooked and deep-fat fried, crisp, moist and astonishingly hot. It would have tasted even better if Bhodi hadn't been sitting opposite Pike.

The Fop's dinner came six-legged, furry, and alive, pinned to a wooden platter by a spike through the middle of its body. Bhodi thought that perhaps Pike had some sort of religious or cultural obligation to kill his own food. But Bhodi stared in mixed fascination and disgust as Pike systematically dismembered the still-squirming creature.

''What do Fop mothers call out the back window? 'Come on in right now, Jimmy, before your food dies'?''

"At least if he plays with his food, it can play back," Parcival said brightly.

Bhodi got through dinner without being sick, which in light of what Pike did with his dinner's torso Bhodi considered an accomplishment of some note. Pike himself helped, distracting Bhodi with stories of his early life in the streets of Calamarod, on the Fop-settled world Fio. The common thread linking the stories was Pike as scofflaw. He cheerfully confessed to petty theft, burglary, grand larceny and assorted frauds and cons, as though none of those things were crimes on Fio.

"I grew up figuring that the only rule that counted was don't get caught," Pike admitted when Bhodi questioned him on it.

"So you joined up hoping the Guardians would change you?"

"Hell, no," Pike said, grinning, "They recruited me because the Ninth needed a good scoundrel."

Parcival shook his head. "Don't believe him. He was arrested in a scam that took half a million from a major landlord in Calamarod."

"And put fifty-three street people into decent housing," Pike added.

"The Fionese government gave him a choice: go off-world or be recycled into pillow covers and hand towels."

"You wound me," Pike said. But his eyes were twinkling merrily.

The waitress, a Fop with whom Pike had been flirting all evening, appeared then bearing the bill for the night's fare. "I'll handle it," Pike said, flourishing a credit chip. Then he reached out and covered Bhodi's right ear, where the translator plug rested. "Kep mardi fractiu noren?"

Smiling coquettishly, the waitress placed the chip in a receptable on her tray, waited until it beeped twice, then handed the chip back. "Jiau."

"Thanks," Bhodi said to Pike as the waitress departed. "This was really good."

"Don't thank me."

"No, I appreciate it. I'd never have known about this place."

"I mean it—don't thank me," Parcival said, sliding the credit chip across the table. "After all, this was on you."

Pike grinned. Parcival laughed delightedly. With a sinking feeling, Bhodi patted dumbly at the empty pocket where his credit chip should have been. Then he snatched up the chip from the table possessively.

"How did you—"

"Oh, I've had it since we went through the security gate at Dock 16," Pike said easily. "I knew you'd want me to help you with the customs. Most junior buys—that's how its done."

"That's a lousy trick," Bhodi said angrily. "You stole my chip. You owe me—how much was it? I don't even know."

"Eighty-six units, not counting a generous tip for the young lady."

"That's a week's allowance! You pig-faced thief, you owe me and you're going to pay me back."

Pike feigned shock. "If you really feel that way, I'll give you a chance to win back what you spent. I hear that Li-hon brought a new game back from Earth on your pickup run." He laughed and pushed his chair back from the table. "Either of you any good at skeeball?"

CHAPTER 11

Pike's little "gotcha" soured Bhodi's enjoyment of the evening excursion. Right up to that moment, Bhodi had felt included and accepted. He knew that Pike was unscrupulous, but Pike was so casual about it and so genial that Bhodi could not make himself judge the Fop harshly.

Then suddenly he became Pike's victim instead of his audience, and the whole business looked very different. Bhodi had never much liked practical jokes, and this was no exception. It wasn't the money. It was the sharp reminder that he, Bhodi, was the outsider.

The incident even left Bhodi with some hard feelings toward Parcival, who not only didn't warn him but seemed to want Bhodi to join an I-was-stung-by-Pike fan club.

"Why are you holding a grudge?" Parcival said when they had a moment alone. "It's nothing personal. I lost all my armor to him on a bet I was sure I could win, and I had to ransom it back. He gets everyone sooner or later."

"That's what Haj said."

"See, you were warned—and he got you anyway. You even had all dinner to notice what had happened. He always gives you a chance to stop him."

"Bhodi shook his head. "I guess I just don't expect people to do things like that."

"That's why Pike's important to the platoon. He helps us remember to think sneaky—not to take things for granted. Anyway, considering how you did with Tivia, he probably figured he'd better get you sooner, because you might not be here later."

"Is that what they're saying?"

"Well—more money says you won't get through your gunnery instruction than says you will."

"Is that so?"

"Yeah. I've got fifty on you making it."

"Thanks—I guess."

Parcival shrugged. "It's a heart bet, not a head bet."

"Why?"

"Don't you know who your instructor is?"

"No. Haj didn't tell me," Bhodi said. With a flash of anxiety, he added, "Don't tell me it's Lord Baethan."

"No. The Lord B. never works with trainees. Doesn't have enough patience with inferior life-forms."

"Who, then?"

Parcival nodded toward a big-bellied figure edging its way toward them through the crowd in the gaming parlor. "It's Pike."

Bhodi stared. "Shit."

The next morning, Bhodi stood outside the door leading to the gunnery range and drew a deep breath. He was trying unsuccessfully to settle his nerves before entering.

Before they had left Dracona, Bhodi had won sixty units from Parcival and Pike in the gaming parlors. That was just about what their share of the dinner would have been, and Bhodi took enough satisfaction in the winning to forget if not forgive the business of the stray credit chip.

But there was still the matter of Bhodi's own harsh words, which he had not taken back. He had decided to apologize at the end of the evening, but lost his chance when Pike unexpectedly advised them that he was staying on Rejia for the night.

The announcement had come just as their taxi reached the flightline, five minutes before the scheduled departure of the night's final shuttle. Pike let Parcival and Bhodi clamber out first, then leaned forward to whisper an instruction in the driver's ear. The driver nodded, and the vehicle lurched forward.

"If you'll excuse me, my gentle companions, a certain young lady in the employ of Hop Zoid's modest establishment awaits my return," Pike had called to them, standing up backward as the taxi rolled away.

"Thanks, Uncle Pike," Parcival had called back, waving.

Pike saluted. "The pleasure if not the profit was all mine. Bhodi Li, sleep well."

There was no chance to say any more, not with the taxi disappearing into the gloom and the shuttle waiting.

Twelve hours later, Bhodi's imagination had turned that innocent parting into an ominous warning. Part of Bhodi was hoping that the young lady's charms had been sufficient to detain Pike on Rejia. But expecting otherwise, Bhodi had come prepared in fighting clothes and full armor, his helmet tucked under his arm.

Voices down the corridor told Bhodi that he would soon have company, and he did not want to be found standing outside a closed door like an idiot. Swallowing his apprehension, Bhodi touched the plate and ducked through the opening that appeared.

A moment later laser light splashed across his right shoulder just below the cop, slicing through the strap that held the armor piece in place. He reacted without thinking, without even feeling astonishment. Dropping his helmet,

Bhodi dove away to the left, and the cop came off as he shoulder-rolled to a crouched position.

He looked up to find Pike standing a half dozen paces away, looking at him down the sight-tube of a long-barreled phaser pistol.

"What—" Bhodi began.

Then he saw the muscles of the Fop's hand flex slightly, and Bhodi instinctively threw up his left arm to protect his face. A moment later the forearm guard fell to the floor, and Bhodi felt a blast of heat through the material of his suit.

Before the heat could become acutely painful, Bhodi sprang up with a spinning move and dashed for the door. He managed three steps before he felt the left cuisse loosen. It slid down his leg and his long strides kicked it against the wall.

He was almost to the door by then. But as he reached for the touchplate, a stabbing beam of laser light from Pike's phaser began to circle it like an electron orbiting a nucleus. To open the door, Bhodi would have to reach into the beam with no more protection than the thin fabric of his gauntlet.

Instead, Bhodi drew back his hand and turned to stare at Pike questioningly. As he did, Pike flicked the energy beam sideways, slicing the straps holding the holster cuisse in place, and Bhodi's last piece of armor dropped to the floor. The floor of the gallery was littered with equipment, like a battlefield after a slaughter.

"You have a bet down on me failing or something?" Bhodi demanded, finding his voice.

"Couldn't find anyone to take it," Pike said, tipping the barrel of his pistol ceilingward. "So I decided to go the other way and cover all the short bets. I got very good odds."

"Then why the target practice?"

Pike made the weapon disappear into his belly pocket.
"I thought we'd get this business of a rematch out of the
way right up front. Just in case you had the same notion
about proving something to me that you did with Tivia."

Outrage and anger bubbled to the top of Bhodi's emotional kettle, released by the knowledge that the moment
of danger had passed. "She at least took me on even," he
snapped. "You might notice I don't have a pistol."

But even as he protested, Bhodi knew that his words
were foolish. The pinpoint accuracy of Pike's phaser fire
had made the point plainly: even armed, there was no way
that he would have been on even terms with the Guardian.

"But you *had* weapons," Pike said lightly. "Or what
was all your work with Tivia about?"

"Right," Bhodi said disdainfully. "I'm going to charge
somebody who has a phaser pointed at me."

"Sometimes your choice is charge them or die—if the
distance to your opponent is less than the distance to
cover."

"That my first lesson?"

"No," Pike said, surveying the litter on the floor.
"Your first lesson is that armor is not invulnerable. Go
see the armorer. He'll issue you replacement straps—and
an Allison B-5 phaser sidearm. When you return we'll
start on the rest of the curriculum."

The Allison pistol was a hand-and-glove fit with the
recess in the holster cuisse. A size-five glove and a size-
six hand, that is. Drawing it was harder, it seemed to
Bhodi, than it ought to have to be. There were two catches
that had to be released to get the weapon free—one on the
cuisse, and one on the pistol's grip.

"They sure don't make it easy to get this out fast," he
complained to Pike.

"And why should they? The quick draw of your Western epics is foolish theatrics. Any warrior who doesn't have his weapon at the ready before he needs it is a fool who deserves to die young.''

"You can't live with a gun in your hand."

Pike's expression darkened. "You can when the alternative is dying with it in your holster. Bhodi Li, your first job is to let go of what you think you know. You know nothing. If you continue to think otherwise, I'm going to lose a thousand units on you and you're going to find yourself back on Earth wondering why you feel light-headed.''

"What's the point? I'll never shoot like you."

"That's not the role planned for you. Look at me, Bhodi. I'm fast for my size, and reasonably agile. But do you think that I can run down a fleeing Arrian, or charge a battle nest? I'm specialized for sniping and fire support.''

"Is that what they want from me? Charging nests of monsters? Is that how you got the vacancy in the platoon to begin with? No, thank you. You can send me back now.''

Pike crossed his arms over his barrel chest. "What is the reason for your ambivalence, Bhodi Li? What has happened to the confident warrior I saw on the recordings Li-hon showed the platoon? What has happened to your boldness? What has happened to your great spirit?''

"That was a game!" Bhodi fairly shouted. "Don't you get it? Jesus, you could have killed me with that business this morning, and this is only the training! I ought to be going to Friday night football games and feeling up Denise at the school mixers. And Parcival—''

"What of Parcival?''

"Do you know he only really acts like a kid when you're around? It's like you're his father, letting him be his own age—''

"I know," Pike said, nodding. "I'm very happy to give

him that. Do you know, when he first came to us he never laughed. He was always serious—always earnest.''

''So he ought to be driving his teachers crazy and looking forward to puberty. What right do you have to take a kid like that and throw him in the middle of a war?''

''Are you going to tell me that he would have been better loved and cared for on Earth? Do you know anything of his story?''

Bhodi hesitated. ''Yeah, a little.''

''Then you know he's where he wants to be.''

''He's too young to make that choice.''

''You're wrong to judge him by his years,'' Pike said. ''He understands the choice. Yes, he may die young. On his next mission, perhaps—none of us ever know when we go out whether we're coming back. But who are you to say that he shouldn't be allowed to make that choice?''

''I—''

''Besides, you don't really care about Parcival,'' Pike pressed. ''You're just using him to avoid talking about something else.''

''I do, too, care. What d'you mean?''

''It's very simple and very obvious. You talk about protecting Parcival so you don't have to admit you're afraid.''

''Hell, yes, I'm afraid,'' Bhodi snapped. ''I'd be an idiot not to be.''

''But are you afraid of failing, or succeeding?''

''I don't know what you're talking about,'' Bhodi sulked.

''No? I think perhaps you'd like to avoid having to face the third refusal. That way you can avoid facing the question of what you're made of, and go back to Earth and recapture the fantasy.''

''The fantasy?''

''You had an image in your mind of what you were. We've taken that from you. You are not the best fighter here, not even the best of the challengers. Can you admit that, or is it too much honesty?"

His chest tight, Bhodi drew a breath before answering. "All right. There are a few that are better."

"To be specific, you currently rank forty-seventh out of fifty-two on the instructors' chart."

"I've only been here ten days!"

"And you've shown us anger, arrogance, impatience and ambivalence about your challenge."

"I worked *hard* on Ja-Nin."

"By your standards, perhaps so. Compared to other students, not so. And it is progress, not effort, which counts here."

"So what are you telling me? Go home? Quit before I'm fired?"

Pike settled on the floor and, with a sweep of his hand, invited Bhodi to do the same. "I'm telling you to examine yourself and decide what it is you want. Only when you know your goal will you have a chance of reaching it."

"That sounds real simple," Bhodi said, sitting back on his heels. "But it's not that easy."

"Then let me try to help. Why did you come here? Why did you make the first refusal?"

Bhodi hesitated.

"Honest answers, now."

Sighing, Bhodi stared up at the ceiling. Then he shook his head. "Jesus, I watched the shuttle blow up on TV at school and I figured that was it for space. And all of a sudden I'm looking down at old planet Earth and there's someone asking me if I want to see more. What else could I say?"

"And now—why do you stay? Now that you know the price of extending your sight-seeing tour."

Bhodi frowned. "I—I don't know."

"Do you want to go home?"

"No. Except sometimes I think, what if something happens to me and there's no one to go back and rescue my family from what they went through when I disappeared."

"If you die, their loss becomes real and their grief valid," said Pike. "Would you take that from them, too?"

Bhodi shook his head. "I guess I didn't think of that."

"Next question. Do you want to become a Guardian?"

"Yes—and no," Bhodi said after a moment's consideration. "Yes, because it would mean something. No, because I don't want to die."

Pike nodded understandingly. "Bhodi—this uncertainty is something that comes on nearly every challenger recruited from a world with no knowledge of the war. Your uncertainty is even stronger because you don't quite believe you can achieve what you reach for, and so are afraid to try."

There was an edge of defensiveness in Bhodi's voice. "What would you think if you'd been beaten as many ways as I have?"

"As I said before, we deprived you of the image you had of yourself. But Bhodi, understand that the reason you're here is that we have an image in *our* mind of what you can be."

"What do you mean?"

Pike leaned forward and rested his palms on the floor. "I'll tell you something you're not meant to know, Bhodi Li. There is nothing—nothing!—that you're being asked to do that you're not capable of doing. The tests you underwent when you arrived assured us of that."

"So?"

"So the question isn't whether you can, but whether you will. Commit yourself, give yourself to this fully, and I'll turn you into a warrior Li-hon and Tivia and even Lord B. will welcome into the platoon. Then you can face the question of staying or going home honestly."

Bhodi's expression was dubious. "You can do that for me?"

"Yes," Pike said gravely. "If you trust me."

Bhodi stared, then began to snicker. "That's funny."

Pike's expression softened, then he, too, started to laugh. "It is, isn't it?"

"All right, Ferthewillihan Pike," Bhodi said, standing and thumbing the releases to bring his Allison into his hand. "Let's do it."

CHAPTER 12

The first hours were devoted to making Bhodi familiar with his new weapon. Unlike the weapon he had been provided for the audition, the Allison was no clone of the standard Photon pistol. Physically, it had a longer, slimmer barrel (the correct term was focus tube, Bhodi learned), a rakish sighting ridge along the top (which seemed a poor substitute for a LED sighting light), and more weight in the grip.

Most importantly, it had a faster response. With the Photon pistol, Bhodi had learned to space his shots a second and a half apart, since the arena's scoring system could deal with nothing faster. That conditioning had to be unlearned. As Pike had demonstrated to him that morning, with the Allison it was possible to get off several effective shots in a single second.

Another part of Bhodi's reeducation was the concept of the effective shot. With the Photon pistol, a hit was a hit was a hit. With the Allison, what Pike called "holding" a target was as important as hitting it. Once the output setting was at maximum, longer holding times were the only way to get more energy on target. And it was concentrated energy, not good targeting, that did the damage.

"If all you manage is to light up your opponent, you might as well not have fired," Pike said. "All you've done is give away your position, like being the first to turn on your flashlight in a dark room."

Bhodi asked about more powerful weapons and was told that the Allison was the most powerful "free" sidearm available to the Guardians. Free in this context meant that it was dependent on its internal source of energy.

But there were heavier weapons in the arsenal, heavier both physically and in the sense of having greater energy resources, and Pike did not neglect them. In fact, Pike made a point of acquainting Bhodi with every personal energy weapon available to the Guardians. There were twenty-six such standard arms, from a two-shot derringer too small to contain a microgenerator and which used expendable piezocapsules instead, to a shoulder-mounted bazooka-like pulse phaser that would have been at home as the main armament on a fighter ship.

Special attention was given to the weapons of choice of the rest of the company. "You need to know what's at your side or your back," Pike said. "But beyond that, you never know when you might need to fight with a weapon pried from a dead friend's hand."

Pike himself carried an Allison with a modified sight, plus two of the tiny derringers. He showed Bhodi how he could conceal the derringers in the palm of his large hands to give the appearance that he was unarmed when he really was quite well defended.

Tivia's sidearm was a Bracke, slightly less powerful than the Allison but a more comfortable fit for her smaller hands. "Not that she likes to use it," Pike added as Bhodi turned a Bracke over in his hands. "If she can get away with it, she tries to go the whole mission without drawing it. Or if she has to draw it, to go without discharging it."

"Seems like that could be dangerous, to herself and the platoon. Pride goeth, etcetera."

"It's not pride. It's tradition, and tradition is Tivia's blind spot," Pike said. "The sergeant's had a few run-ins with her about it."

The other three members of the platoon formed its heavy-weapons team. With his size and strength, Li-hon was a natural for the pulse phaser and its relatively small 140-pound backpack power unit. Lord Baethan literally *was* a weapon—a Celtan-designed three-beam phaser was built into his right hand, so that all he needed to do was raise it and think the command to fire. The triphaser drew on the same power source as did Lord B. himself, which meant that as long as he could fight, he could fire.

True to form, Parcival had designed a unique weapon for himself—basically a modified Allison mounted on an articulated arm atop Parcival's hard-shell electronics-crammed backpack. Using an autotargeting system, the weapon could fire hands-off from any position in a 180-degree rainbow arc from over Parcival's right shoulder to over his left, at any azimuth from minus twenty degrees to plus fifty, and in any direction.

Though the autotargeter was still a hair too slow and a bit too easily fooled for any of the others to adopt the weapon, it did free Parcival's hands to operate the jammer-scanner "black boxes" he wore on his right wrist and left forearm. Real-time intelligence and electronic dirty tricks were Parcival's most important battlefield contributions.

"There's a lot to learn," Bhodi said dubiously as they wrapped up their armaments survey.

Pike patted his shoulder. "Not more than you *can* learn."

Pike was true to his word. In three short days, he gave

Bhodi what he needed most—he gave him his confidence back. And he did it by making war a game again.

It started with target practice on a marvelous high-tech firing range. But to get to it, Bhodi and Pike had to transport down to the planet. Like all of the gunnery training facilities, it was located in Rejia's sterile outback, part of a cluster of low, sprawling buildings that reminded Bhodi of a GM automobile plant he had once seen during a family vacation.

Bhodi's concept of a firing range was based on what he'd seen in police dramas—shooters lined up on one side, targets lined up on the other, like a bowling alley for guns. But the range was shaped more like a baseball field, only larger. The angle between the "foul lines" was 120 degrees instead of ninety, and the curved back wall was easily 250 meters away, too far for even a Mike Schmidt or a Kirk Gibson to hit one out.

But there was only a single shooter's station, more or less where home plate would have been. In the first exercises, Bhodi stood on the shooter's station and potted a series of stationary red disks located at a distance of twenty-five meters, evenly spaced in an arc from left field to right. When he had proved himself at that distance, a new set of targets popped up from the floor at fifty meters, then a hundred, then two hundred.

It was easy shooting. The Allison was lovely and cooperative, and Bhodi quickly learned to trust and admire it. There was never an errant shot or a misfire Bhodi could blame on the weapon. There were few enough Bhodi needed to blame on himself, for the sight was true and the weapon steady in his hand.

But it did not stop there. In the following days, Pike systematically added complications that elevated the level of the challenge. Bhodi was presented with a mixture of targets at assorted ranges and instructed to shoot the closest ones first. He was offered targets that popped up momentarily from the floor or flashed diagonally across the range.

In time, all variables were exploited. Exercises were conducted in the equivalent of full midday light, twilight dimness, and moonlit gloom. The targets themselves shrank, reduced in increments from the size of a human head to the size of a clenched fist.

"Do you know, I'm *good* at this," Bhodi said to Pike after slicing a half-second off his time in the ten-target speed test.

"Yes, you are," Pike agreed. "How does it feel?"

"It feels good. Except there's something wrong."

"What's that?"

"Well—it's too easy. They're not shooting back, for one thing. Which means I'm standing here flat-footed, something that'll never happen in combat."

"Very true," Pike agreed. "And I've been waiting for you to say something about it."

The next day, Bhodi was brought to a second gunnery arena, adjacent to and the same size as but outfitted very differently than the firing range. The arena floor was broken up by waist-high sand-colored walls into dozens of trenchlike boxes of assorted sizes.

"The dueling range," Pike said. Halfway across the arena, a claw-fingered, four-armed monster rose up from behind one of the walls and pointed a pistol in Bhodi's direction. "Your opponent."

Bhodi stared. He remembered the creature from Lihon's presentation on board *Fraanic*. "Not real, I take it."

"A simulacrum. But programmed with the fighting reflexes of the real thing, as best we know them from our combat recordings."

"Does it have a name?"

"Around here we call it Warriarr—double 'r' on the end, a little pun. What the species calls itself we don't know. We've never captured one. We've never even recovered a body." Pike paused. "But then, that's true of most of the species that make up the Arrian Alliance. Anyway, these beasties are the ones we run up against most often."

"Cheerful thought."

Pike shrugged. "I'd rather fight Warri than the Bugs or the Dogs."

Bhodi had little trouble deciding which species Pike was referring to. The squat canyon-jawed Dogs and bulging-eyed Bugs had stayed in his mind as vividly as the Warri. "Why?"

"The Bugs are faster than Warri, and awfully good shots. And the Dogs are just plain tough. They keep coming long after you think they should have gone down."

"How do you match up when you run into all three at once?"

"Happily, the Arrians don't mix it up much. There's no telling whether it's a racial thing—pride or prejudice—a problem of discipline, even something religious. Maybe the Bugs think the Dogs smell bad, and vice versa. Anyway, more than half the Arr squads are made up wholly of Warri. The rest are usually all one species, plus a Warri commander and maybe a Dog."

"So the Warri run the show."

Pike nodded. "There's even some thought in the Intelligence branch that the Warlord of Arr is Warri."

"It would seem to make sense, considering," Bhodi agreed.

"Whoever the Warlord is, I hope he never wises up and starts sending out mixed squads. Right now, our battlefield organization is one of our big edges. In pure size and strength, the Qeth are the only Guardians who match up with a Warri, a Bug, a Dog, or a Destructor. And the Celtans are the only allies who match up in toughness. Hell, the Warri don't even wear any armor in combat."

Shaking his head in disbelief, Bhodi asked, "How can battlefield organization overcome that?"

"Because it takes advantage of *our* advantages. We're faster—even I can outrun anything but a Dog. And we're more versatile. Like I told you before, we're all different. We all have things we do better than anyone else. It's a good team—a good platoon—or at least it was."

"Was?"

"I don't know what we are, now. We haven't fought as a platoon in three months—just pairs. Me and the kid, Tivia and Lord B."

"Why?"

"I guess because Li-hon's not ready to take us out again. Do you know how casualties go in the Force? A platoon can go six months or a year without losing anyone. Then somebody goes down and it seems like you'll lose a replacement or two and another regular before you find the fighting sync again. That's why he wants you, Bhodi. He thinks you're the missing piece that will pull us back together." Pike gestured toward the simulacrum. "Ready to find out how you match up?"

Bhodi unclipped his Allison. "Sure."

"Then put your helmet on," Pike said. "Warriarr's weapon *is* real."

The dueling range's deadly game of hide-and-seek had two objectives. Once you had your enemy located, you tried to keep him from moving. Once you had him pinned down, you tried to keep him neutralized. Ideally, you maintained enough fire superiority to be able to keep your head up and the whole contested area in view.

In that kind of pop-up, snap-shot combat, it was difficult to take out your opponent. Unless Bhodi froze while exposed, his helmet would keep a head shot from being a killing shot, though he could be temporarily blinded by the dazzle if he took one in the faceplate. And Warriarr's single ailette, projecting up from his right shoulder like a metallic wing, made a perfect head shield when he turned sideways to the line of fire.

In the first minute, Bhodi learned that he was quicker than Warriarr. If he was already up when Warriarr poked his head above the wall, Bhodi could usually duck down before the simulacrum got off anything other than a blind prayer shot. Or Bhodi could stay up and try to burn some energy around or through Warriarr's ailette to his unprotected skull.

The danger for Bhodi was when Warriarr would stay up, letting Bhodi hold target harmlessly on the ailette, and then return fire left-handed around the edge of the shield, like a counter-punching boxer. Warriarr fried Bhodi's faceplate twice before Bhodi learned to pull off of the shield and pop a blast inside the little angle formed by the edge of the ailette and the wall, right under Warriarr's pointed chin.

It was a tough shot, but when Bhodi could make it work, it invariably sent Warriarr ducking for cover, giving Bhodi the heads-up advantage. It also seemed to make Warriarr angry. After Bhodi's first chin shot, Warriarr disappeared momentarily, then rose up to his full height, offering Bhodi a free shot at his whole torso—if Bhodi cared to face the murderous crossfire from the twin pistols Warriarr held in both his lower hands.

Bhodi declined the offer, retreating hastily behind his own wall to reconsider his options. *What was it I told David? The best cover is cover you don't depend on for too long—* He didn't know if he was allowed or expected to do what he was considering. *But then again, Pike didn't hand out any list of dos and don'ts—*

The moment there was an interruption in the laser fire raking the top of the wall, Bhodi sprang up and dove forward over the wall into the next trench. Scrambling along on hands and knees, he went as far to the right as he could.

He paused there a moment, listening, wondering where Warriarr was and where the simulacrum thought he was. A peek would tell him the first, but the price might be betraying the second. And if he was going to expose himself, he wanted to gain something for it. Tensing his muscles, he drove himself upward and forward over another wall.

In mid-dive, he caught a glimpse of Warriarr. Warriarr likewise caught a glimpse of him. Laser fire blazed overhead as Bhodi hit the floor, making the material of the walls sizzle and pop. Bhodi ignored the angry noises and scooted to the left as fast as he could. When he ran out of trench, he went for his Allison. Praying that he had the angle, he rose up, the Allison blazing away.

His first shot caught Warriarr on his unprotected right lower shoulder blade, just below the crisscross straps that held the ailette and two sheathed throwing knives. It was not a critical area, but as Warriarr turned in surprise—and perhaps in pain—Bhodi caught him full in the face with a shot that he held until Warriarr toppled over backward and disappeared.

Vaulting the walls like a hurdler now rather than a high jumper, Bhodi approached the "corpse" cautiously.

"Well done," a voice said from behind.

Bhodi turned. It was Pike, reentering from the observer's booth.

His face still a blank, Bhodi looked back to the inert

form of the simulacrum. Then a broad grin spread across his face as he holstered the Allison.

"Yeah," he said happily, more to himself than to Pike. "Well done."

CHAPTER 13

To Bhodi's disappointment, two days later his gunnery work was unexpectedly interrupted when Pike and Parcival were called away on a mission. Their departure was so abrupt that Pike left Bhodi no assignments and made no arrangements for him to continue his work in the combat gunnery center.

"Sorry," Haj said with a shrug. "There's one reservation in advance, for tomorrow in the firing range. I can let you have that, since your instructor made the request. But a challenger alone has to wait in line behind all the other instructors for training time, and I can tell you right now that someone's going to snap up the slots Ferthewillihan was using."

"The firing range? There must be some mistake," Bhodi protested. "I'm way past that. What about the maze room? That's where I really need to be."

Haj shook his head. "Impossible. The maze room is fully scheduled—and I would not be responsible for placing you in it without proper preparation in any case."

"Why? What goes on there?"

The training supervisor frowned. "If Ferthewillihan told

you about the maze room, I don't understand why he didn't explain its purpose."

"I didn't hear about it from Pike. I heard about it from another challenger, down at the gunnery center." Seeing Haj's look of disapproval, Bhodi added, "I wasn't snooping. He was scheduled to go in that afternoon and was nervous. Made him chatty."

Haj regarded Bhodi sternly. "Challengers are to discuss their training only with their instructors. Each program is unique, and all that can come out of comparing one with another is confusion."

Scanning down a list on his display, Haj continued, "I see that you were next scheduled to work with Parcival on field maintenance of arms and equipment. I am reluctant to seek a substitute for Ferthewillihan unless that becomes absolutely necessary. But as you haven't begun working with Parcival, I could possibly seek a replacement among the other Guardians on-station—"

"No," Bhodi said quickly.

"Very well. I understand your preference to take instruction from within the platoon—"

That was not it at all. Bhodi did not want to be sidetracked into the kind of tedious detail that "field maintenance" promised to include, especially in light of whom he had been scheduled to study with. But Bhodi said nothing to correct the misimpression.

"What I would suggest is that you approach Tivia about some supervised practice. Ja-Nin is a discipline, not a tool. It needs your constant attention, and I'm afraid you have been neglecting it in your enthusiasm for gunnery."

"No to that, too."

"What?"

"Look, let's be straight," Bhodi said. "I know that that's not what Li-hon wants me for."

"Why do you think that?"

Bhodi realized belatedly that he was in danger of putting Pike in dutch with the training supervisor, and he tried his best to cover up. "Look, it's just obvious that's not my role on the team. I'll never be good enough to take on a Destructor or a Dog hand-to-hand. And what even Tivia would do against six limbs is something I'd like to know. So why should I spin my wheels over Ja-Nin when I could be sharpening up on what I *am* good at?"

"Is that how you see it?" Haj asked stiffly.

"Yeah."

"Then I suggest you speak to Sergeant Li-hon about your problem," Haj said. "Perhaps he will be able to find a solution."

"Can he get me into the maze room?"

"Li-hon is the most respected instructor of strategy and tactics in the entire Force, as well as the most senior," Haj said in a curiously emotionless voice. "As such he may request priority time in any training facility for any of his students."

"Which means me, right? He's my sergeant, so he must be my S&T instructor."

"He is when he says he is. It's customary for a challenger to master all other disciplines before beginning his study of strategy and tactics. I doubt very much that Li-hon will find reason to make an exception in your case."

"But he could, right? So I *will* go talk to him."

"Do that," Haj said. "I am sure he will have interesting things to say."

The great lizard lay curled on his side in the corner of the room, cushioned by the shredded padding of his nest.

"Nar-lex-ko-li-hon."

He blinked in the darkness of his quarters. "Yes, First Guardian?"

"There is a problem—"

Li-hon sighed. "A new problem or an old problem?"

"A new problem which concerns an old problem."

"That would be Bhodi Li."

"Yes. Haj-til-ko-van has submitted a supervisor's recommendation for preemptory dismissal. It is most strongly worded. He said the boy is completely unfit for further training. He blames Pike."

Li-hon struggled to a sitting position. "Let me see the rec."

A full wall of the chamber flashed into light. Li-hon quickly scanned the symbols projected there. "Haj is too harsh," he pronounced. "Pike did what was necessary."

"It is beyond refutation that humans lack discipline and motivation. In that Bhodi has proved himself no exception. Is there not now enough reason to think that it is Parcival who is the exception, and give up the effort to find warriors among the human population?"

"They show more than enough motivation when they know the reason why," Li-hon disputed.

"And hasn't Bhodi Li been told of the Arrian menace? Is he ignorant of the threat to his homeworld?"

"The threat is still not real to him. He still thinks that he will somehow be safer going home."

"Then the problem is an immature mind. He is unable to grasp a need greater than his own."

"Yes. But that, at least, is open to change."

"Then you intend to dispute Haj-til-ko-van's recommendation?"

"Yes. Please record it."

"Haj-til-ko-van will be displeased."

"That doesn't matter. Not to me, anyway."

"You understand that this makes you a partner in Bhodi Li's challenge."

"In my mind, I always was," Li-hon said. "Where is Bhodi now?"

"En route to see you. Now in Corridor Gold, Section Yellow, about two minutes away."

"Can you delay him until I get out? This conversation will go better in the platoon room than here. And that way I won't have to make a scene about being disturbed in my quarters."

"I will delay him at the section boundary touchpoint."

It seemed to Bhodi that everyone and everything was determined to squelch his enthusiasm for continuing his training. Bhodi was eager to prove himself, to face the next hurdle and transcend it. But the First Guardian had stolen his instructor, Pike had run off and forgotten him, Haj had been uncooperative right up to the point when he located Li-hon for Bhodi, and now the boundary sensor at the Section Green entry point was refusing to acknowledge his presence and pass him through.

"Nothing to worry about," the boundary-keeper said as an intermittent stream of traffic in both directions passed through without difficulty. "It happens sometimes. Just keep trying."

Bhodi did, touching his bracelet to the sensor every time there was a break in the traffic. Each time, the response lamp above the saloon-door-style gate stayed dark, glowing neither red to pass him through nor violet to turn him aside.

More than five minutes slid by before he finally connected with the station's traffic management computer and passed through the touchpoint. But his frustration did not end there. When he reached the Command Quad and found what he thought was the doorway to which Haj had given him directions, the door did not open for his brace-

let, and there was no response to the chime that he presumed sounded inside.

So either Haj had been in error, or Bhodi was in the
wrong place. It was hard to be sure which, because Bhodi
could not read all the symbols beside the threshold. The
numerals were right—21—but maybe the rest didn't say
Nar-lex-ko-li-hon, or Command Quad. For all he knew,
the symbols said Laundry, High Voltage, or Employees
Only.

Why do they have to have such a damned complicated
alphabet, Bhodi fumed as he retraced his steps to the
section boundary. Forty-two letters and it all looks like
sloppy Chinese. If they can give me this translator plug,
why can't they give me some sort of computer contact lens
that'll make it look like English to me? Because they like
to make everything harder than it has to be, that's why—

At the touchpoint, Bhodi filed a where-is query with the
boundary-keeper. He was told that Li-hon was in the Ninth's
platoon room, located two levels down along the Section
Green's outermost corridor.

I wonder where he'll be when I get there, Bhodi thought.
Are we playing spacetime hide-and-seek?

But he forgot his annoyance when he reached Level 10.
It was not physique alone, but something in their faces that
told Bhodi that the people he saw in the corridors were
Guardians. He had moved into Intellistar's inner world.

That impression was confirmed by Bhodi's first glimpse
of Platoon Row. He stood looking down the length of a
long, dimly lit lounge. Most of the seating areas were
empty, but near the far end a half dozen Guardians in
combat suits were clustered together. The left wall was
solid glass—or whatever the Alliance used in place of
it—and looked out to space and a spectacular starscape. To
the right was a line of widely spaced thresholds inter-

spersed with large, colorful emblems hung like medieval heraldry on the wall.

As Bhodi started along the row, his eyes scanned ahead and found an emblem he knew. It was the same symbol that appeared on the sleeve of Li-hon's fatigues—the emblem of the Ninth Platoon. He stopped at the door nearest it, paused, then touched and went inside.

Li-hon was seated in the hexagonal pit that dominated the center of the room, perched on a stool and poring over the glowing display lying on the table at the center of the pit. But Bhodi almost didn't notice Li-hon, for his eye was drawn immediately to the back wall. The upper third of the wall was filled with portraits of individual Qeth, Celtans, and other Alliance species. There were more than fifty portraits in all, three rows across and a third of a fourth row.

"Ah, Bhodi," Li-hon said, rising up. "Haj said you might be trying to find me."

"Who are they?" Bhodi asked, still staring at the wall of faces.

"That's the Ninth's Wall of Honor," Li-hon said, turning to look that way himself.

"You've got your own Hall of Fame," Bhodi said approvingly. Then he added, "I guess there's a lot of tradition here. The platoon's had a lot of heroes."

Li-hon turned back to Bhodi. "I'm afraid you misunderstand, Bhodi Li. These are faces of the warriors who fell wearing the insignia of the Ninth. We remember them for their service to the Light, not individual deeds. Character makes a soldier. Circumstance makes a hero."

Bhodi gulped. Heroes were one thing; dead heroes something entirely different. Suddenly he wasn't quite as eager as he had been.

"I understand you are interested in beginning a study of strategy and tactics," Li-hon continued.

"Uh—yes. I know—I mean Haj told me it's not the usual procedure—"

"I think it's time," Li-hon said, "and that is more important than any fossilized habits."

"Uh—thanks." That was easy, Bhodi thought with some puzzlement. What was Haj talking about?

"I have an hour's work remaining," Li-hon said. "We can begin when it's completed."

"I could meet you at the transporter station—"

"No. Wait outside in the lounge until I'm ready."

"Okay. But shouldn't I go get my armor?"

"You won't need it," Li-hon said and settled back on his stool.

Bhodi was kept waiting in the lounge long enough for the space station's slow spin to bring Rejia into view twice. During that time, the only person Bhodi saw that he knew was Lord Baethan, who passed within two yards of him on his way to the platoon room. Predictably, the cyborg failed to notice or acknowledge Bhodi's presence; he might as well have been part of the chair he was seated in.

Shortly after Lord Baethan left, Li-hon appeared and called Bhodi in. He offered him a seat at the pit table— which Bhodi later learned was called the battle board—and then settled back on his stool. It was then that Bhodi learned the reason he did not need his armor: His studies with Li-hon were to begin not with a duel or an ambush, but a conversation.

"How closely have you studied the campaigns of Earth's great strategists—Alexander, Hannibal, Caesar, Sun Tzu, Genghis Khan, Napoleon?" Li-hon asked.

Bhodi almost laughed. "Well—I've heard of most of them. Military strategy isn't exactly a core subject in my high school."

"And yet it has always seemed to me that it would be, since your species seems to be constantly at war," Li-hon said. "Very well. What do the words 'strategy' and 'tactics' mean to you?"

Bhodi considered a moment. "I guess strategy is what you're trying to do, and tactics is how you try to do it."

"Reasonable. What, in your perception, are we trying to do?"

"We, meaning the Photon Alliance?"

"Yes."

"Well, whip the Arrians, of course."

"But how will we know we've won? What is our specific goal?"

Bhodi felt like he were being quizzed by Mrs. Martini about an assignment he hadn't read, and was enjoying it just about as much. "I guess to find the Arrian equivalent of Intellistar and bomb it to bits."

"No. You are confusing strategy and tactics." He touched a colored area on the battle board and a picture appeared in the center of the surface. It was the crater-surfaced mushroom-shaped space station he had seen in the *Fraanic* briefing. "This is called Scarrcastle—"

"How'd you get the picture?"

An intelligence intercept. We have several spy buoys operating inside Arrian space."

"They probably have them here, too, huh?"

"Not inside this system," Li-hon said. "Our sweeps here are very thorough. But elsewhere—probably. Communications are scrambled on the presumption that they could be intercepted. But again you deflect me to a tactical question. The point I was making is that we know the location of the Arrian command base. We have never attempted an assault on it, and never will."

"Why? It seems to me the fastest way to end the war."

"Scarrcastle lies deep in the midst of the Darkness. To

die in Darkness is to become separated from the Light forever. The First Guardian will never order her warriors to face that risk.''

No wonder you've been fighting this war for two hundred years, Bhodi thought. ''Then what *are* you trying to do?''

''The Force's sole strategic goal is to end the Arrian interference with the spread of the Light.''

''Don't you want to go all the way—wipe them out and take their worlds, too?''

''No,'' Li-hon said firmly. ''The Arrian homeworlds are irredeemably contaminated by the Darkness. We have no interest in them. Our mission is to the worlds that have never known Light or Darkness.''

''All right. I have the picture.''

''Then consider another question. What are the elements of victory?''

''Uh—get there first with the most warriors?''

''Ah. You know more of your strategic tradition than you admit.''

''Huh?''

''That was Nathan Bedford Forrest's prescription for victory. He was a general in your American Civil War.''

''I didn't know that,'' Bhodi admitted. ''It just came off the top of my head.''

''So much the better, since I would have had to convince you that Forrest was wrong,'' Li-hon said. ''Listen carefully, Bhodi Li—no soldier, no force, is invulnerable. Neither size nor number nor experience nor firepower in itself is enough to guarantee victory. The winner of a combat is the one who best exploits his own advantages and conceals his own weaknesses.''

''That makes sense.''

"Does it make sense, too, that a warrior must therefore know his advantages and weaknesses?"

"Yes—"

"And he must see both clearly, without the exaggerations of pride and the illusions of ego?"

"I guess—"

Li-hon jabbed a meaty finger in the direction of the Wall of Honor. "Then start clearing away the veils from your own eyes, Bhodi Li, if you hope to be a Guardian," he said sharply. "I myself have hung fifteen of those portraits. I have no wish to hasten the time when my own joins them. I look forward to fighting beside you, but not enough to go into battle with a fool."

"I'm not a fool," Bhodi said, bristling.

Li-hon shook his head. "That remains to be seen."

CHAPTER 14

There was no mistaking the fact that the rules had changed. Bhodi's time was no longer his own. Li-hon owned it, and Bhodi learned quickly that Li-hon did not believe in leaving assets idle.

Promptly at seven on the station's thirty-hour clock, Bhodi appeared at the platoon room for the first of three daily sessions with Li-hon. Nine-half found him in the Ja-Nin room, warming up for a full-armor combat bout with an opponent of Li-hon's choosing. Then it was hurry back to Li-hon for the second session of the day.

At fifteen he got an hour's break, which always seemed half as long as it should be and was usually dedicated to a quick meal and a waking nap in the handiest comfortable spot. At sixteen he reported to K'ieasl of the Seventh Platoon for instruction in field maintenance. Then at eighteen-half he bounced down to Rejia for work with the Allison.

Twenty-one meant back to the platoon room one last time for what always seemed to be the most complex tactical problems of the day. Then, just when he was sure that his brain was going to explode from too much thinking, he was shipped off to Haj for a brisk bit of work on

his general conditioning program. By twenty-five he was
free, but by that point he had little interest in anything
more demanding than a meal and falling into bed.

But when he tried complaining to the other challengers,
he was answered with consternation instead of commisera-
tion. Not only had they been on comparable schedules all
along—by *choice!*—but also they envied him the chance to
study individually with Li-hon and Haj both. After hearing
the same refrain from three different would-be sympathiz-
ers, Bhodi decided to just shut up and endure.

But he was nevertheless convinced that he *was* being
singled out for special treatment, and not in a good sense
of the word. For example, his Ja-Nin bouts were full-
armor free-contact matches, complete with referee. Though
Guardians occasionally conducted demonstration matches
in that format, no one else trained that way. And even if
that had been routine, Bhodi simply wasn't up to it. Through
the first week, he usually left limping and always left
hurting.

Then there was the matter of the audience. From the
first day, his matches played to a dozen or more spectators—
station staff, other challengers, even an occasional Guardian. And though they were not overly verbal, they seemed
to be there to root against him. Bhodi suspected that this
was Haj's lesson for Bhodi, a public answer to the question "What good is this?"

And lesson it was. Bhodi did not mind being seen, per
se. But he hated for anyone to see him being whipped
quite so thoroughly. His first two opponents were Qeth,
and he could do virtually nothing with them. Each weighed
more than five hundred pounds, their skin was as unyielding as shoe leather, and even their glancing blows threat-
ened to break bones. All Bhodi learned from those
encounters was how to stay out of reach.

His next three opponents were all Ikthalarians. They had

a deceptive kind of wiry strength, and their long armspan gave him fits. Even so, he handled himself reasonably well—though not well enough in any instance to walk away feeling like the winner. But his skills were unquestionably improving each day. The primary reason was his determination not to be victimized by the same maneuver twice. That and the audience, whose eyes he could never quite forget and whose amusement he could never quite make himself deaf to.

The handling of his Ja-Nin sessions was not the only sore point. Every trip down to Rejia for gunnery practice was a goad in his side, for he was always scheduled for the firing range, dueling range, or one of the three skirmish zones outside on the planet's surface. He was never penciled in for the maze room. It was not even mentioned.

True, he himself hadn't raised the subject with Li-hon. That was partly fear of repeating his mistake with Haj, and partly his certainty that Li-hon would arrange it at the appropriate time—which Bhodi was certain would be soon—without being reminded or cajoled. So day after day, Bhodi potted hexagonal targets or played tag among the rocks, all the while chafing at the bit for a chance to show what he could do in the training center's ultimate test.

He did not understand why Li-hon was waiting, and yet dared not ask for an explanation. For a brief time, the return of Ferthewillihan Pike to Intellistar gave him a reason to hope for a change. Pike, at least, was someone he could risk being honest with. But although Parcival took over from K'ieasl, Pike seemed content to leave things as they were, in Li-hon's hands. Pike confined himself to an occasional visit to the observer's booth, and even then seemed to avoid any contact more direct than a smile or a wave—almost as though he had been ordered to stay away from Bhodi.

But for all the pain from the Ja-Nin and the frustration surrounding his gunnery training, Bhodi's greatest trial was the time he spent with Sergeant Li-hon. Li-hon's version of strategy and tactics instruction embodied everything Bhodi hated about school—dusty history, pedantic theory, and endless talk-talk-talk. Except it was worse, because he could not hide among his classmates and thereby avoid joining in the game called pretend-to-be-interested.

Movement of forces. Economy and concentration of force. Geometrical strategy. Blockade. The strategy of interior lines. Reconnaissance. The strategy of exhaustion. Cohesion and dispersion. Flank assault. Double envelopment. Cordon defense. There seemed to be no end to Li-hon's catalog of military lore.

It was not just the onslaught of new words. Bhodi was constantly struggling to grasp points that his instructor seemed to think were self-evident. Li-hon would say something like, "The goal of the tactics of attack is to create a conviction of defeat in your enemy."

The first thing Bhodi said was always wrong. "I thought the goal was to kill as many of theirs as you can while losing as few of yours as you can," he had offered on that occasion.

Then came the contradiction. "Numbers are less important than the will to fight. Small armies have often routed larger ones."

Thinking he now understood, Bhodi would respond with what he thought was a comment of agreement. "Sure—by inflicting more casualties."

Almost inevitably, Li-hon would destroy the illusion of understanding with his next utterance. "Casualties are frequently the result of defeat, not its cause. You must understand, Bhodi Li, that the defeated force in virtually every battle in your history or mine still retained the capacity for useful resistance, in many cases even the capacity for victory. They were overwhelmed not by the enemy, but by a sense of hopelessness. So the goal of the tactician is to crush spirit, not bodies.''

Then the obligatory sucker question: ''So how do you do it?''

''By striking where the enemy thought it impossible for you to strike—and by making them feel their losses.'' Finally the inevitable metaphor, which Li-hon seemed to expect Bhodi to remember as a distillation of the discussion. ''Suffering is measured not by the size of the wound but by the acuity of the pain.''

It all meant something to Li-hon, but none of it meant much to Bhodi. He wanted to know how best to handle a Warri in open ground, how the Arrians used their Dogs, what a Destructor did when startled—practical knowledge that Bhodi could take into battle, the profit of the hard lessons learned by those whose pictures hung facing them.

But an eavesdropper listening in on a session would be hard pressed to decide which or even what kind of war was going on in the universe outside the room. It was all so maddeningly abstract, Bhodi complained in silence. *Give me something real—*

The only truly enjoyable part was the trickery Li-hon could do with the battle board. At least once during every session, its black-glass surface dissolved into invisibility, and the table became a hexagonal tank containing a flawlessly detailed miniature of a battle scene.

The simulation was three-dimensional like a model, its colors exaggerated like a computer graphic. Bhodi did not know whether it was a hologram, film projection, animation, or simple magic. Whatever the means, the battle board invited Bhodi to size up a specific strategic situation, make predictions or even tactical decisions, and then see his instincts tested as the battle was played out by the tiny figures and war machines. His instincts were frequently good, at least where the span of time involved was short.

But aside from that, there was little pleasure and less promise of pleasure. For three weeks, Bhodi bore it all stoically. He understood that he was in the pressure cooker, his grit and commitment being tested. When he felt his resistance rising, he checked the impulse to revolt with the reminder that Li-hon was the best, or remembered Pike's assurance that he could do anything that would be asked of him.

Then came the day when he rushed into the Ja-Nin arena a few minutes late and found the black-metal figure of a Celtan waiting for him in the match hexagon.

"Wait a minute," Bhodi started to complain to the referee as he crossed the line. "This isn't fair. He must be a Guardian. Celtans don't even go through training. They just have it all programmed in—"

Ignoring him, the referee waved his right hand in the signal that meant *Engage*. A moment later, the Celtan hit Bhodi from behind, taking him to the floor, and the bout was underway.

Bhodi bounced up from the blind-side attack furious. "Come on, then, you sideshow freak," he snapped, circling in a crouch. "Come on, I'm going to pull your goddamn plug."

The Celtan sprang forward and unleashed a roundhouse kick. Adrenaline flooding through his body, Bhodi was ready and dove under the kick to one side. His legs lashed out in a scissor chop that found the hard metal of the Celtan's boot plates and sent it sprawling awkwardly facedown on the floor.

Bhodi was on his feet in an instant, fists clenched, eyes full of fury, awaiting the Celtan's next charge in a crouch. But the cyborg stayed on the floor, rolling to its side and signaling to the referee.

"Yield," it said. "My right hip joint has been hyper-stressed. I am unable to continue."

For a moment, Bhodi was enraged that he was to be denied a chance to compound the Celtan's injury. But as the referee stepped in and Bhodi stepped back, he heard the applause—applause from the audience that had been invariably cool to his efforts up till then. He turned towards them and saw for the first time friendly faces among the gallery. In answer, he allowed himself a proud smile and a clenched fist of triumph.

A short time later, he overheard a whispered conversation as he waited for a lift:

"Is that him?"

"Yeah—that's the kid who beat Kil Vander at Ja-Nin."

"*He* beat a Celtan? I don't believe it—"

"Broke Vander's leg and left him lying there. Did it like it was the easiest thing in the world."

"So what's he still doing here?"

"Shoot, I don't know. Ask the First. And ask her soon. I've got to fight him next week."

The lift came, and the duo fell silent as they crowded in with him. But Bhodi did not need to hear more. All of the suppressed thoughts of the last three weeks were coming to the fore. *What* am *I still doing here?* Bhodi repeated to himself. *I want to hear Li-hon answer that one—*

If Li-hon had been appraised of what had happened that morning in the Ja-Nin arena, he gave no sign of it. "There is a work, the *Tactica*, written by your Emperor Leo the Wise of Byzantine, which contains some interesting ideas," Li-hon began.

"Really?"

Ignoring or missing the sarcasm, Li-hon continued. "He recommends the use of fraud and bribery—" Then he stopped, realizing that Bhodi was making no move to join him at the battle board. "Is there a problem, Bhodi Li?"

"Yeah. I'd like to know how much longer this is going to go on."

"Until you're ready for your third refusal."

"And when will that be?"

Li-hon rested his thick forearms on the battle board. "Explain yourself. What urgency is there? What timetable are you failing to meet?"

"Bro'nech came here the week after I did—"

"Correct."

"He took his third refusal and joined the Eleventh two days ago."

"Also correct."

"But that's not right. I've been here longer."

"That means nothing."

"It means that you're promoting people ahead of me. People who're no better than I am. I beat Bro'nech three times in the dueling room, and almost beat him in Ja-Nin."

"He was ready. You are not—"

"Why not? What are we waiting for?"

The question failed to deflect Li-hon from the point he had begun to make. "Your protest is triply inappropriate. We have also dismissed challengers who have been here longer than you. There is no meaning in the order of ascension. Also, Bro'nech came to us with his potential more completely realized than you did. He needed only polishing. You need molding. And most important, you are not challenging for the Eleventh. You are challenging for the Ninth. The standards other sergeants may set for their platoons are meaningless here."

"So it's you that's holding me up. Well, what am I not doing right? What am I not doing that you think I ought to be?"

"The truth is, I'm reasonably content with your prog-

ress.'' He grinned his disturbing toothy grin. ''So is Pike.
He's already collected half a thousand units from those
who bet against you.''

''If I'm doing so well, why can't you tell me when this
will be over?''

''It will be over when you've learned what you need
to.''

''What, more games of cavalry and castles?'' Bhodi
said, waving a hand toward the battle board. ''What good
is any of it? Do you know what I did today? I beat Kil
Vander at Ja-Nin. I beat a Celtan. I beat a Guardian-class
fighter.''

''Perhaps. Some observers credited the floor and an
awkward fall with the victory.''

''They're wrong,'' Bhodi snapped. ''I made it happen.
Look, there's no one in the training section better than me
with an Allison. Everybody knows it, and after today
everybody's going to know they've got to respect me
hand-to-hand, too.''

''The respect of your peers is important,'' Li-hon said.
''To you. But it makes no difference to the Arrians whether
you're held in high regard or in contempt. Your skin burns
the same either way.''

''Why are you trying to make me think I'm not ready? I
know I am. I know what I can do.''

''I'm not trying to puncture your confidence, Bhodi Li.
I'm trying to push you off your pendulum in the middle of
a swing, so that you see yourself as neither invulnerable
nor helpless. The truth is somewhere in between, and until
you grasp it, you can't be trusted in combat.''

Bhodi would not hear it. ''What's my ranking?''

''What?''

''You know what I mean. On the instructors' chart.
Where do I stand?''

Li-hon frowned and growled deep in his throat. "There is no such scoring."

Bhodi's face wrinkled in puzzlement. "But Pike said—"

"I can fully believe he did. But there is no such scoring. How could there be? Each challenger, each vacancy, each commander's need is different. How can they be compared?"

"He lied to me?"

"If he felt the reason sufficient, he might have."

Shaking his head, Bhodi said, "It doesn't matter. I don't need to hear it from anyone else to know I'm right."

"Then what *do* you need?"

"A chance!" Bhodi fairly shouted. "Jesus, I don't understand you people. You want me and you don't want me. You talk about the psychology of defeat and then do everything you can to bust me down. You get me primed for fighting and then won't let me fight."

"What, in your opinion, should I be doing?"

The anger left Bhodi's face and was replaced by a grim determination. "For starters, you can let me have a crack at the maze room."

"You do not even know what you are asking for."

"Then tell me."

Li-hon studied Bhodi closely before answering. "The Arrians do not wait until they have crystals in hand to begin their preparations to use them. They land their teams on disputed worlds and unclaimed worlds and build warrens, quite extensive when time permits, where the crystals can be taken to be reprogrammed. They need time and they need secure cover to be successful."

"Because you'd just destroy the crystals if you had the chance—better to lose a crystal than lose a world."

"Yes. So again and again we find it necessary to go underground and clean out the warrens to retrieve or destroy a captured Photon crystal. The catacombs of your Photon arenas are an echo of this need.''

''And the maze room—''

''The maze room pits a single challenger against an unknown number of living opponents inside an Arrian warren. Your opponents know the maze. They know what your objective is. They know that you have to come to them.''

''That's no different than going after the base goal in the game.''

''You're wrong. It's very different.''

''It doesn't matter. I want it. I want to try. Give me a chance to find out. The worst that can happen is that I'll discover you're right—that I'm not ready.''

Li-hon took forever to respond, as though wrestling with a decision of tremendous weight. ''Very well,'' he said at last. ''I'll arrange it.'' *But that isn't the worst that can happen*, Li-hon thought. *The worst that could happen would be that you win.*

CHAPTER 15

Bhodi Li had expected to see very little with his first glimpse of the maze room, because he thought the great volume of the arena would be fully taken up by the structure of the maze. When the moment for that first glimpse arrived, he indeed saw very little, but for a very different reaason. The chamber was virtually empty, like a new house where the furniture hadn't been moved in yet. There was almost nothing to see.

With Li-hon standing at his elbow, Bhodi scanned the surprising scene. The "floor" was hard-packed soil the color of sienna, and the walls were cleverly painted in a way that made the illusion of a planetary surface extend to the horizon. The landscape was featureless save for three gently sloping mounds, like great waist-high anthills, located in a triangle near the center of the chamber.

"That's the Arrians' favorite design," Li-hon said, following his gaze. "They use it everywhere the terrain allows. Very low profile. We had to develop special sensors to detect them. As soon as we did, they started scattering phony ones all over the map, with all three entrances booby-trapped."

So that's what the dark patches are, Bhodi thought.

Each mound had a black wound—more like a hole angling down into the earth than a doorway—on the side facing the center of the triangle. The sight reminded Bhodi vaguely of the storm cellar in *The Wizard of Oz*, minus the doors. The rest of the warren was underground, unseen and unknowable.

Defensively, the whole arrangement was both elegant and intimidating. A warrior standing in the entrance and facing outward had the protection of a foxhole and the sightlines and battlefield command of a machine-gun nest. Even if the defenders were driven down into the tunnels, any entrance could be covered by a crossfire from the other two.

"Nasty," Bhodi said.

"Yes. At the real warrens, only two of the three entrances are booby-trapped."

Bhodi swallowed hard and tried to keep his discomfort off his face. "So when do the nasties show up?"

"They're already inside."

He knew better than to ask how many. "I get the approach for free?"

"The Arrians prefer not to fight on the surface when they can avoid it," Li-hon said. "Why should they? May I see your weapon, please."

"Yeah," Bhodi said, handing him the Allison. "Why should they? So how can you tell which of the entrances is safe?"

Li-hon checked the power reserve and the output rating, then handed the weapon back. "You can't. Good luck, Bhodi Li." Then he walked away and disappeared through a doorway that made it seem as though he were stepping off the edge of the world.

For a long minute Bhodi stood stiffly in place. *This is a psyche-out*, he thought tersely. *He wants me to get jelly-knees and go back into my shell. I can't believe they can't*

*give any better briefing on cracking a warren than 'You
can't.'*

Bhodi looked up in the direction of the hidden observer's booth and its invisible wide-field cameras. *I'll bet he
packed the booth, too. He wouldn't tell me, because he
wouldn't want to give me any extra motivation. Haj and
Pike and the First Guardian—maybe the whole damn
platoon, come to see Bhodi's last hurrah. Son of a—*

Turning his attention toward the triple mound, Bhodi
tried to steel himself for the challenge ahead. *Two out of
three chance I don't even make it past the entrance. Great
odds.*

He realized that his mouth was dry and his heart racing.
Scared? he taunted himself. *Yeah. Scared of putting my
head down one of those holes and getting it fried off.*

*Everything they ask me to do, they already know I can
do,* he reminded himself.

But this time, Pike's assurance could offer no comfort.
*They didn't ask me to do this—I asked. I'm the one who
said I was ready, not Li-hon. And now I've got to do it, or
I can't face them again. But how? How do you beat these
kind of odds?* For a long moment, he wavered on the verge
of following Li-hon out the exit, laying down his Allison,
and going home to safe, tame little Montclair.

It was something else that Pike had said that rescued
him, a comment he had made after Bhodi had won his
fourth straight live-opponent duel. "You know what I like
about you?" Pike had said, clapping his hands on both of
Bhodi's shoulders. "You fight dirty."

At first, Bhodi had wondered if he should take offense.
But Pike hastened to explain that he meant Bhodi wasn't
afraid to expose himself to a hit to gain an edge or achieve
an objective.

"I like the guys that come back with phaser tracks all
over their armor," Pike had said. "The armor's there to

protect you. If you never take advantage of that, you're
not getting out on the edge where you ought to be. These
types that come out of a firefight without so much as a
scorch mark on their fighting suit, you can have 'em. Give
me the guys who fight dirty.''

That's how you beat the nasties, Bhodi thought. *You
fight dirty. That's the way you used to play when it was
just a game. And win or lose, that's the only way to play
it now—*

That decision cleared the emotional cobwebs from Bhodi's
reasoning, and immediately he found himself following a
more productive train of thought. What kind of booby trap
would they use? Hydraulic walls to crush you? A dead-end
with a five-meg phaser cannon firing straight up at you?
Razor-sharp spikes that shoot out of the ceiling?

No matter what the trap, Bhodi realized, an invading
force could find out which entrance was the real one
simply by being willing to sacrifice two warriors. Unless
you designed a booby trap that was so well hidden nothing
gave it away until it was too late for the would-be invader
to relay his discovery back to his platoon mates. A warrior
goes down into one of the holes and is simply never
heard from again.

Yes—it would have to be something quiet. No explo-
sions, no odd noises. It would have to be something tidy,
to avoid having a clutter of dead bodies to warn the next
one in. And it would almost certainly have to be something that was automated, tripped by sensors of some sort.
They wouldn't want to isolate part of their fighting force in
dead-end false tunnels, not when they could be needed
elsewhere.

So what, then? A slippery ramp with a vat of acid at the
bottom?

Bhodi wished he had some sort of flying camera to send

in first. Even if they fried it, a glimpse of what was past the entrance would be worth the loss. *If only I didn't have to go in first and find out the hard way—*

Then he realized that, in fact, he didn't have to go in first. He had no partners, no equipment to spare and the landscape was barren, but there were other resources. Specifically, there were grapefruit-sized light globes arrayed all across the "sky"—the ceiling of the arena.

Backing off a few steps, Bhodi pulled on his helmet and raised his Allison above his head. With three pinpoint blasts, he burned away the supports that held three of the globes. They dropped loudly to the surface, dimmed rapidly and went out, but did not shatter. The last of the three rolled to a stop just inches from his booted foot.

"What's he doing tearing up the arena?" Haj demanded, coming up out of his chair in the observer's booth. "*My* arena. Li-hon, I insist you put a stop to this right now."

"I said he would have a chance," Li-hon said. "Sit and watch."

"I won't tolerate it. No one has ever done anything like that before."

"I agree," Li-hon said. "And I'm interested to see what use he makes of them. Sit down, Haj. This is only the beginning."

His plan vague but complete, Bhodi scooped up the faintly warm globes and started toward the warren. He circled around the back of the nearest of the mounds, cradling the lights in the crook of one arm and holding the Allison at the ready with his other hand.

Then he started up, as though on his way to play king of the hill. Three steps up, he was on his knees. By the time he was at the top, he was lying prone.

When he peeked over the top, he could see slightly

inside the entrances of the two other mounds, but nothing of the entry to the one he was on. Holstering his Allison and leaving two of the lights perched precariously on the top of the mound, Bhodi squirmed forward on his belly until he was close enough to the entryway to stick his head out and look down into the tunnel.

There he paused for a moment and bled off some of the incredible tension he felt with a hearty exhalation. Then he touched his helmet controls, activating the image amplifier built into its faceplate, and stole a peek inside.

He had not expected to be shot at, and was not. Why should they scare him off at the door, when patience would bring better opportunities? But he did not see much. His head motion plus the sudden transition from the well-lit arena to the dark catacomb made the amplified image ghost like a badly tuned television.

Tensing himself, he took another, longer look. This time he saw an empty earth-walled corridor an armspan wide and barely fifteen feet long, terminating in a T with a cross corridor.

There are two hiding places, he thought as he withdrew. *They get to hide around the corners, and I'm backlit against the sky. So easy they ought to be ashamed.*

But that assumed that this was the true entrance, and not one of the sucker traps—an assumption he wasn't going to make without testing. He poked his head out past the edge for a third time, and when the image of the corridor stopped ghosting, hurled the light globe down into the darkened tunnel.

It bounced once against the floor, and a moment later four bluish beams of phaser fire flashed from below and intersected in the air above the globe. Bhodi resisted the impulse to duck back out of sight. He watched as the globe bounced twice more, strangely untouched by the continuing phaser blasts, arced back toward the floor a third time—and then vanished. There a momentary hum, a crackling noise, then silence.

Bhodi blinked, then backed quickly away from the edge. It took him a moment to realize that the globe had dropped right through the floor as though nothing were there. That in fact nothing was there. Part of the floor was missing, its absence hidden by some clever trick of lighting and coloration. The automatic phasers had missed their bouncing target because they were meant to miss. They were there only to drive an intruder along at an appropriately reckless pace.

Climbing down from the first mound, Bhodi circled clockwise to the next. As expected, the second entryway appeared identical to the first. He repeated his test, sacrificing a second globe. This time nothing happened. The globe rolled to the bottom of the ramp, bumped the back wall of the cross corridor, and came to a stop unmolested.

A second-man-through booby trap? Bhodi wondered. *Smart systems that won't get fooled the same way twice? Or the real entrance, with hidden snipers that are cool enough to wait for the real thing?*

Instinct more than reason persuaded Bhodi that he had in fact found the real entrance. But he felt little joy at the accomplishment. *They know I'm up here now. And they'll hear me coming, slipping and sliding on that dirt chute, and fry my butt on the way down.*

He retreated to the back of the mound to consider his situation. *Just a moment,* he thought. *Just a moment of surprise is all I need—one trick they're not expecting. Just enough to get me to the bottom in one piece.*

Then, in a moment of insight, he realized that he had the trick in hand—had practiced it a hundred times in his own house (and been reprimanded countless times by his Mom for doing so). The steep-sloped entryway was like a stairwell, and he had already perfected the fastest way of going down a flight of stairs—

Bouncing up, he scooted in a sweeping lefthand circle to the area between the mounds. He lobbed the third light globe down the mouth of the second false entryway, then started running toward the real entryway. When he reached the shadowed threshold he leaped toward the darkness, catching the top of the opening with his hands and used that as a leverage point to swing his feet forward.

He was flying feetfirst down through the chute, out of control. If he had guessed wrong, he was going to end up flat on his back at the bottom, the breath knocked out of him, staring up at the psuedo-Arrian who was going to have the pleasure of dispatching him.

But he had not guessed wrong. His entry into the chute had tripped some sensor, and as Bhodi dropped toward the bottom a figure stepped out from the right and started firing up the ramp. But Bhodi was not where the warrior expected Bhodi to be, and the shots missed low. A moment later Bhodi's boots caught the warrior in the thorax, driving his body backward and snapping its neck forward.

The collision drove the guard all the way to the wall, where it was sandwiched momentarily between rocklike earth and a human projectile. With something to push against, Bhodi turned his fall to the floor into a twisting roll and came up with the Allison in his hand. He burned his opponent's chest pack with his first shot, and only in the light of its exploding circuitry did he see that his opponent was Qeth, disarmed, and quite unconscious.

One—

Bhodi did not linger. He snatched up the fallen warrior's sidearm with his free hand, tested it with several shots down the dark passage to the left, then started himself down the passage to the right with both weapons at the ready, like a two-gun sharpshooter from a four-horse Western.

He went thirty steps into a corridor so dark that even the image amplifier couldn't capture enough light to provide a sharp view ahead, then slowed as a feeling of terrible apprehension began to haunt him. Something was wrong. It was as though the sound of his own footsteps had changed—

Suddenly his unarmored right elbow was seared by a phaser blast that came out of nowhere. He twisted toward what he had thought was a wall and dropped to a crouch, ready to return fire if only he could find a target.

As if in answer to his unvoiced plea, lights came on all around him. In an instant, he saw that he had blundered into a small chamber with several exits, and glimpsed motion in one of them. In the next instant, the brilliance of the amplified light turned his vision all to white. It was as though a superpowered camera flash had gone off inches in front of his face. He was blind.

On internal compass alone, he spun away and scooted back the way he had come, skidded into a baseball slide, and flattened himself belly-down on the floor facing back the other way. He fired at random down the corridor with his Allison, hoping to drive back anyone who had followed, all the while fumbling with the switch for the image amplifier and praying his vision came back soon.

Then Bhodi realized that it was the helmet itself that was still blinded, the display circuits destroyed by the sudden peak. He slapped the release on the chin strap, shook the helmet off, and found himself looking up at the gaunt figure of an Ikthalarian edging toward him along the wall, a Bracke in its left hand.

They started firing at the same instant, but Bhodi had two weapons and a better angle. He held the Ikthalarian's sensor pack in his sights until it exploded in a shower of sparks. When that happened, the Ikthalarian lowered his weapon, shook his head in self-disgust, and sat down along the wall.

"All yours," it said, gesturing toward the chamber where Bhodi had been blinded.

"So's that," Bhodi said, rising and pointing to the warrior's weapon. "I'm starting a collection."

The Ikthalarian surrendered the Bracke reluctantly, and Bhodi returned his own sidearm to the holster cuisse so that he had a free hand for it. Then he started cautiously down the corridor. The fierce white lights were still on, illuminating not only the chamber itself but also a fair distance down each of the five connecting corridors that branched off it. All five appeared to be empty.

But there was a sixth exit from the room—a triangular hole in the floor that looked like the hole left in dough by a cookie-cutter. Bhodi crept up to the edge, fired at random down into the hole, then leaned out and peered over the edge for a quick glimpse.

The hole led to another chamber below. The floor dividing them was more than two feet thick, and the floor of the second chamber was another ten feet below that. At first there seemed to be no ladder, but then Bhodi spotted a pattern of toe-cuts in the wall of the lower chamber. He could see little more of what awaited below—just a small section of the floor lit from above and his own shadow inscribed in the splash of light.

Bhodi looked up, scanning the branch corridors again, then systematically began to shoot out the rectangular lights illuminating the upper chamber. When the last one winked out, both the upper chamber and the lower were in darkness.

I knew there had to be a reason they were leaving the lights on, Bhodi thought. *I go down that funky ladder with*

*my back to them, spotlighted, and they sit in the dark and
fry me.*

But Bhodi did not plan to cooperate. He waited an
interminable minute for his eyes to adjust, then slipped off
the edge and dropped lightly into the lower chamber.

A beam of blue fury buzzed past Bhodi's head, close
enough to vaporize a few flying strands of blond hair. He
shoulder-rolled to the left and fired back in the direction
the bolt had come from. Each blast of phaser fire dimly lit
the room—far vaster than the upper chamber—in an eerie
light.

Fire and move. Fire when moving. They dueled in
darkness, circling, trying to anticipate each other's moves.
Each tried to use the other's fire as a targeting aid, which
led to short fierce exchanges and long periods of silence
and darkness. Bhodi took hits on both legs, right thigh,
left shoulder, and midback, none serious. He did not know
what he gave in return.

It seemed like the only way the stalemate would end
would be if they bumped together by accident and stran-
gled each other. Then Bhodi got a flash of inspiration.
Stripping one of the straps from his holster cuisse, he
looped it around the grip of the Bracke. Laying the weapon
on the floor, he snugged up the strap against the actuator,
and the weapon began to fire.

Immediately, the unseen enemy began to fire back.
Bhodi rolled twice to his left, into the darkness, then
sprang to his feet. For a count of one thousand, two
thousand, three thousand Bhodi ran away from the Bracke
and toward his opponent as fast as his legs would carry
him. Then he skidded to a stop, dropped to one knee, and
aimed his own Allison and the one taken from the Qeth at
the exact spot from which his unseen enemy's phaser
bolts were appearing.

There was an animal squeal, and the other phaser winked

out. A fraction of a second later, Bhodi heard the thud of something striking the floor. Bhodi kept firing until the lights came up and an end-of-match chime began to sound.

His opponent was a Riknoid and in obvious pain, kneeling and holding its right hand. Its weapon was lying in the center of a splatter of blood. Uncertain of his obligations, Bhodi took one tentative step toward it. But before he could decide whether his help would be welcome, three medical-section types dropped through the hole and hurried to the injured fighter's side.

Bhodi backed away then and retraced his steps through the now fully lighted warren to the entrance. When he reached the surface, he found Li-hon walking across the arena toward him.

"I won," Bhodi said quietly as they came together. "I'm ready."

"You won," Li-hon agreed. "But you're not ready."

"I want my third refusal."

"No."

"But you said—"

"I said I would give you a chance to show what you could do. I did, and you did. Now we continue to work on what you can't do," he said. "Go back to the platoon room. I'll be there when I can be. You've left me with a couple of injured Guardians to look after first."

And then he brushed past and left Bhodi standing there alone in the empty arena, his mind empty and mouth open, unable to quite believe what had just happened to him.

CHAPTER 16

The voice of the First Guardian broke the silence in the nearly deserted platoon room. "Nar-lex-ko-li-hon."

The lizard grunted. "I've been expecting to hear from you, First Guardian."

"Then you understand it is time for an accounting of your stewardship of young Bhodi Li."

"I do."

"Following the maze test last week, Bhodi Li did not report to you as ordered."

"No."

"He then feigned illness to escape two full days of training."

"True."

"Since emerging from his isolation, he has missed thirteen training sessions in nine days—seven with you, five with Haj-til-ko-van, and one with Parcival."

Li-hon's forehead wrinkled. "When was that last?"

"This morning."

"Parcival hadn't notified me."

"Parcival is attempting to locate Bhodi Li and resolve the matter on his own," said the First Guardian.

"Attempting to locate? Don't you know where Bhodi is?"

"Yes and no. Bhodi Li is somewhere in Dracona."

"Oh."

"He has not even bothered to offer an excuse for these most recent absences."

"That's also true."

"Before we consider its significance, can you explain why you have allowed this behavior?"

Li-hon sighed and stretched his massive right leg. "Because I don't know what else to do."

"Explain."

"He's a human! Is there anyone anywhere on this station who understands how they think? What would you have me do?"

"Bhodi Li must follow orders or be sent home."

"Why exactly should he follow my orders?"

"Because you are the sergeant of the Ninth Platoon, and he is a challenger for the vacancy in that platoon."

"That's the answer from our point of view. But what about from his?"

"I fail to see why there should be a difference."

"So did I, at first. But there is. He wasn't sent here by his planet's government, like most of us. He's here on his own. A volunteer, taking part as far as he has for personal reasons."

"He was told of the threat to the Light and to Earth."

"He's not yet one with the Alliance. And Bhodi feels no spiritual identification with his planet, or moral obligation to his species as a whole."

"If this is true of humans generally, then there is little hope for their survival irrespective of the Arrian menace," said the First Guardian.

"I know that all too well. It's the same sickness that nearly destroyed my people," Li-hon said somberly.

"So we cannot expect Bhodi to act out of duty. But it is not clear to me how Bhodi's behavior serves even his selfish interests."

"It doesn't. In my estimation, he now believes that we mean to never allow him his third refusal—that he'll never be a Guardian. He's begun to blame us instead of himself for his failure."

"He is likely right, on both counts. Your decision to allow him to attempt the maze room appears to have destroyed him."

Li-hon twitched his tail. "I didn't expect him to win. That was the whole point—to drive out the arrogance coming in the wake of that fluky victory over Kil Vander. To teach him that he had more to learn."

"You should have anticipated the possibility of his success and its consequences."

"It shouldn't have happened." Li-hon smacked the top of the battle board with one meaty fist. "I had three of the best Guardians on-station fighting as the black force. He had no peepers, no squealers, no partner, and no experience. I didn't figure he had better than one chance in a thousand of beating the warren."

"How do you account for the fact that he did? There appeared to be little chance involved in this victory, as opposed to the Vander matter."

"It's my fault."

"The responsibility is yours. But it seemed to me that your black force defended the warren very poorly."

"It seemed that way to me, too," Li-hon said glumly. "They were in too much of a hurry. The defender has all the advantages. They didn't exploit them the way they should have."

"Have you analyzed why?"

"I did better than that. I had a pointed discussion with them about their performance."

"And?"

"And they agreed they had done poorly."

"You are being obstinate."

Li-hon folded his hands and rested them on his abdomen. "Look, it's not entirely their fault. They're all top fighters, but we're not talking about maze players of the stature of Calder Quinn or Jo-let-jin. Bhodi would never have beaten a team that included either of them, even in a fairer fight. My team had only been in the maze on defense a half dozen times between them."

Li-hon rapped the point of his jaw with his fist in a gesture of self-reproach. "I was in too much of a hurry myself. I should have done a more thorough job of prepping them. Or waited until I had a stronger Arr force on-station."

"You do not need to protect your Guardians from me, Nar-lex-ko-li-hon. Tell me what you learned."

Li-hon flicked his tongue against his front canines restively. "The big problem seems to have been that they knew who the invader was going to be—"

"Outrageous. Who broke security?"

"Everyone and no one. Tongues wag. It doesn't matter. They knew it was Bhodi, and they were eager to put him in his place. Too eager. News of some of his antics have reached the ears of the Guardian community, you see—"

"I'm aware of the stories in circulation."

"Then you understand their motivation—professional pride."

"Yes—the Guardians have their own arrogance. And it was a factor in their performance."

"Yes," Li-hon said. "I underestimated Bhodi to some degree, but they underestimated him even more. And that helped him beat them."

"Very well," the First Guardian said. "I accept your

explanation of the incident. What is your explanation of Bhodi Li's present behavior?''

"I believe the term humans use is 'sulking.' "

"And what is the cure for sulking?"

"Sulking isn't the problem," Li-hon said. "I said that he wanted to become a Guardian for personal reasons. That's what has to change. He wanted to feel important. He needs to want to *do* something important. Then he'll be ready for his ring."

"How do you propose to effect this transformation?"

Li-hon sighed. "It may already be too late. I thought it would have happened already. I thought it would come with exposure to you, to this place, to the rest of the platoon. I thought he would realize how serious this is. But nothing seems to reach him. All I've managed to do is alternately frustrate and frighten him."

"Have you showed him battle recordings from the war?"

"I have."

"What was his reaction?"

"The fact is, he seemed to have no lasting reaction at all," Li-hon said. "I don't understand it."

"Yes," said the First Guardian. "That is what I would have expected. Bhodi Li is handicapped by the entertainment modalities of his homeworld."

"Oh? How?"

"The visual arts are used for fiction on Earth—"

"Blessed light—are they that ignorant? The visual arts should be reserved for that which is either true or taken-as-true."

"Clearly they do not understand the seductive power of the illusions they create. Bhodi Li has seen so much fighting and so much death that was not real that it is difficult for him to fully credit what he sees now."

"Yes," Li-hon said thoughtfully. "It makes sense. And it explains a lot. It explains why he constantly puts himself first—because only his own feelings and own danger are real. And it gives me an idea—but you're not going to like it.''

"Tell me your idea, Nar-lex-ko-li-hon, not what I'm supposed to think of it.''

Li-hon raised his folded hands up under his chin. ''I want to take him out on a sortie and let him see with his own eyes what we're fighting. It's the only thing now that can shock him into maturity.''

"I cannot sanction awarding a ring to Bhodi Li on the basis of such faint hope.''

"I'm not asking you to give him his ring.''

"You would allow him to participate in our great mission before he has earned his Guardian's ring?''

"For this one, I would make an exception.''

"This is more than an exception. It is completely without precedent. What do you see in him that can justify such measures?''

Li-hon's voice was solemn and vibrant with emotion. "He is the missing element that will make the Ninth whole again.'' He paused. ''And me whole, as well.''

"What do you mean? In what way are you injured?''

Li-hon smiled faintly. ''Haven't you noticed, First Guardian? Surely it's not lost on you that I haven't been on a sortie myself for half a cycle, since Marika Krill was killed. It's been easy to arrange—no partner, so much administrative work, so much demand for me as instructor, the Sixth and Fourteenth fighting so well in our sector.''

"Those are valid reasons.''

"I know they are,'' Li-hon said. ''But the real reason is I'm tired inside. I need someone like Bhodi, someone with his enthusiasm, to make me want to fight again.''

It was the First Guardian's turn to pause. ''Very well, Nar-lex-ko-li-hon. Let us discuss it.''

•   •   •

Parcival hated going to Dracona alone, and for several good reasons. He was treated better as Uncle Pike's companion than he ever was on his own. The completely shameless mating manners of the Ikthalarians made him feel vaguely uncomfortable, and Pike always seemed to manage to steer him away from such sights.

But the most important reason was more practical. He was too short to see through the ubiquitous crowds, and without Pike there to sweep the way clear, Parcival had trouble even moving through them. With his build, he got the worst of every bump and jostle, and sometimes felt like he was being swept along like flotsam on a biotic tide.

All of those problems made searching for someone particularly vexing. He had been in nine of the gameries so far, and though a few people thought they had seen Bhodi Li, Parcival had not really picked up his trail yet. It was beginning to look as though it would be a long search. Then he entered Alia's Arcade.

There was a noisy argument going on in one corner of the sunken gaming floor, but the crowd was thinner than in most of the establishments he had visited. That and the raised entryway were the key to Parcival spotting Bhodi, perched in the player's cage—something like the basket used on the back of an elephant— of the K'arli Hunter machine. With a sigh of relief, Parcival paid the pass fee and made his way across the gaming floor to him.

Bhodi's attention was fully focused on the targets appearing on the wraparound screen, and he did not notice Parcival standing to his left. So when a brief break between rounds came, Parcival spoke up.

"What are you up to, Chris?"

Bhodi took one sideways glance to confirm who had spoken, then shouldered the heavy dart thrower. "Forty-two hundred points. Not too good, huh? But at least there's no one telling me I'm not allowed to score any more."

"That isn't what I meant."

The action picked up, the screen filling with needle-toothed K'arli on the wing, and Bhodi did not answer. But when a fanfare signaled the end of the game, Bhodi slid down, turned away from the machine, and replied, "I know what you meant. You want to know why I cut out on you and came down here."

"Not exactly, Chris. It's pretty obvious what you're doing. I'm just not quite sure why."

"I've got reasons enough," he said offhandedly. Then his gaze narrowed quizzically. "Say—why are you calling me Chris again?"

Parcival shrugged. "Just seemed like you've made your choice about which name really fits."

"Hey—what are you trying to say? Are you calling me a coward?"

"No. I guess I'm calling you a dropout."

"Listen, it's not my fault."

"No? Then it wasn't your idea to come down here instead of showing up to work with me?"

"Don't bust my chops."

"Hey, I don't take it personally," Parcival said. "I figure it's a compliment that you didn't get bored with me before this. I guess you've been cutting out on other people for two weeks now."

Bhodi sighed. "Do you want something to drink? If you really want to talk about this, it's going to take a while."

Parcival scanned around the room. "Do they have anything here that we *can* drink?"

"No—but The Eclectic across the street does," he said, nudging Parcival and pointing toward the door. "I've been there twice already today."

●   ●   ●

The contents of Bhodi's glass looked like cream soda but tasted like the birch beer it was advertised to be. The untouched glass in front of Parcival contained a chocolate milk that he had pronounced undrinkably bitter.

"I'm not going to fight their prejudice anymore," Bhodi was saying. "I don't know why you can't see it. They don't like humans, and they aren't about to let any more of them into the Force. I thought Li-hon was on my side, but something's happened to him, too. Maybe he's been pressured by the others."

"You don't understand anything about the Alliance," Parcival said, shaking his head.

"I suppose you're going to educate me."

"No," Parcival said. "I don't think you're ready to hear anything that disagrees with what you're already sure is true."

Bhodi leaned forward and rested his elbows on the table. "Look, I thought we were friends. Or at least starting to be."

"Then stop treating me as the enemy. Didn't I level with you when we picked you up? Wasn't everything I told you a hundred percent true?"

"Yeah," Bhodi acknowledged. "You were—and it was."

"Then listen to me. There's no prejudice. None that counts. Sure, Tivia can't stand men, and Lord Baethan can't stand full-biologicals. But neither one of them would let that stand in the way of beating the Arrians. What they want from you—"

At that moment, the clear crystal in Parcival's copper-colored Guardian's ring began to pulse, and the ring itself to chirrup like a cricket. "That's okay," Bhodi said, slumping back in his chair. "Go on. You've got something more important to do."

"That's the signal for a check-in, not a muster," Parcival

said, craning his head until he spotted the com hood, a fixture in every establishment in Dracona. "I'll be back."

In three minutes, Parcival returned to the table. "I've got to go upstairs."

"I figured—"

"They wanted to know if I'd found you. If I had, they wanted me to tell you that you've been assigned to the Ninth as combat aide for the sortie we're about to go out on."

"I don't under—"

"They also said that if I hadn't found you, not to look for you anymore—that they would send you home when you finally decided to show up." Parcival folded his hands over his chest. "So, Chris, tell me—have I found you?"

"What are you talking about?" Bhodi said, bouncing up. "This is what I wanted! I don't understand it, but I'm not going to ask. Let's go."

CHAPTER 17

Since they were dependent on the Dracona shuttle for their return to Intellistar, Bhodi and Parcival were the last to report in. They found that the rest of the expedition and even their own gear had already been transported up to the Ninth Platoon's carrier, *Zephyr*. The blunt-nosed twin-tailed star fighter was in a high geosynchronous parking orbit around Rejia—as Bhodi learned, one jewel in a glittery necklace ringing the planet.

"I thought our ship'd be here at the docks," Bhodi said as they checked in at the transport station's touchpoint.

"There's not enough room down here for all of the platoon carriers and couriers and scouts," Parcival said, accepting the travel orders offered up by the station-keeper. "But there's more than twelve hundred slots up there, a quarter of a degree apart."

There was a minor backlog at the outbound transporter, and they took their place in line. "You have that many ships?"

"Some of them are the primary defense platforms, some are decoys. But there's two or three hundred other ships up there at any given time," Parcival said. "All the armed ships, like our *Zephyr*, are part of the secondary station defense. You didn't think the Arrians were leaving us alone here out of courtesy, did you?''

"No—"

"You should see what it looks like when the First Guardian calls a scramble drill and a hundred or so ships all fire up out of orbit in the span of a few minutes." Parcival turned to the transport engineer. "Two for the *Zephyr*. She's in slot 914."

"Happy hunting," said the engineer, saluting as they moved past him into the chamber. "May the Light shine."

When the blue cocoon faded, they were aboard the *Zephyr*, standing amidships at an intersection of two passageways. Parcival stepped forward and slapped the intercom bar on the nearest wall.

"Tech Spec Parcival Pike, reporting in," he said, then moved aside to make room for Bhodi.

Bhodi hesitated for a moment, then reached out and pressed the bar. "Combat aide Bhodi Li, reporting in."

The answering voice was Li-hon's. "About time, you two," he said impatiently. "Come forward to the bridge."

When they reached the triangular bridge, similar to but larger than that on *Fraanic*, Bhodi learned that the full platoon had not been assigned to the sortie. Tivia and Lord Baethan had been called that morning to back up a force fighting on a planet called Marchia, leaving only Parcival, Pike and Li-hon available.

I wonder if that's why they brought me along, Bhodi thought. *Pinch-hitter for the Ego Twins. Except they can't expect me to fill both their shoes. Why did they bring me? What's a combat aide do, anyway?*

Even without a full platoon, *Zephyr* was carrying a full load. Unlike on *Fraanic*, there was a crew of three, wearing smoke-colored uniforms and manning the bridge stations. Though Li-hon was clearly the final authority on board ship, it was the Riknoid Li-hon called Captain Yier who took *Zephyr* out of orbit and set her on course for the Cavalon system.

"We can't be everywhere at once," Parcival explained later. "We need someone to fight the ship while we're doing our job on the planet. Captain Yier's a good one—he's been the Ninth's carrier pilot for almost fifteen cycles."

Also aboard was a squad of what Li-hon called the Regulars and Bhodi came to think of as the junior varsity. They wore identical pale-blue light-armor fighting suits with the spectral disk emblem of the Alliance on the sleeve, carried Brackes and Allisons, but wore no Guardian's rings. Bhodi had not known such a force even existed.

"Is that an option for me, if I don't make it into the Guardians?" he asked Parcival.

"No" was the answer. "They're selected and trained by their own planetary governments, not by the First Guardian. Occasionally a Regular is allowed to challenge for the Ring, but we don't send them our rejects."

According to Parcival, the Regulars performed the sort of support roles that would otherwise have divided the platoon's strength or consumed its time unproductively—security, sentinel duty, mop-up operations.

"Most of the time it's the Regulars who escort crystal teams," Parcival said. "In equal numbers, they're no match for the Arrians. And you sure wouldn't ask them to go after the Warri on their own turf. But they do a good job of backing us up. You might say we're the offense and the Regulars are the defense."

Clearly, like *Zephyr's* crew, the Regulars were considered part of the team, an extension of the platoon. If there had been any doubt of that in Bhodi's mind, it was dispelled when both Captain Yier and Corporal Mlas, commander of the Regulars, were included in the sortie briefing Li-hon conducted when *Zephyr* was barely an hour out of Rejia.

The briefing was held in a compartment on the lower deck, with the six participants seated around a battle board. "This sortie is a rescue-and-retrieve for the courier *Majestic*," Li-hon told them. "She was carrying a crystal team and a phalanx of Regulars on a six-stop seeding mission in the Kalath sector. *Majestic* made her in-system report at Cavalon and hasn't been heard from since. Ditto her escort, the sloop *I'olhlm*."

"How many crystals was she carrying?" Parcival asked.

"Three. Cavalon was the fourth stop, which means that she was carrying three prime crystals when she hit the system."

"No alternate?" Parcival pursued.

"No. The prime failed on their second stop and they needed to use it."

"Cavalon is awfully deep into our zone for this to be the Arrians," Yier commented.

"I'd like to think so, but it's hard to imagine any other reason. Two ships going silent means four transmitters have to fail all at once, or some accident has to take both ships out simultaneously. Pretty long odds on that."

"One in sixty-three million on the transmitters alone," Parcival said.

"Li-hon's right," Pike said. "It's pretty gutty of them to come in that far, but it has to be the Arrians. The killer is that we're not going to find them hanging around when we get there."

"It has all the signs of a snatch-and-run," Li-hon agreed. "There's been no evidence of any warren-building in the Kalath sector since we pushed them out eight cycles back. I hate to say it, but we're probably looking at two toasters and a lot of bodies to pick up—"

"They like to wait until the team is on the ground, then fry the escort," Parcival whispered, leaning close. "Then they crack the courier open in orbit, take the crystals, and skip—"

The whisper was either too long or too loud to pass notice. "Problem, Parcival?" Li-hon interrupted.

Parcival straightened up on his stool. "Just putting Bhodi in the picture."

"He can speak, can't he? If he's got a question, he'll ask it."

"Yes, sir," Parcival said sheepishly.

"As I was saying, about the most we can hope for is that some of the ground team is still alive. But if by chance the crystals are still around, we're going to go after them."

Pike shook his head in disgust. "Won't happen, curse the dark. We're gonna be late to the dance."

"There's always a chance *I'olhlm* got in a few licks before she went down," Li-hon said. "In any case, we're going on standard battle prep as of the end of this briefing— combat diet and power sleep. Captain Yier will get us to Cavalon late tomorrow."

"Twenty-half ship time," Yier amended.

Li-hon nodded. "Any questions?"

Bhodi raised his hand. "I've got one. What's my role?"

Captain Yier snickered, and Pike studiously avoided looking in Bhodi's direction. "Your role is to do what you're asked, when you're asked, to the best of your ability," Li-hon answered.

"Can't you give me some idea what that's likely to include?"

"No."

"I'm not asking for promises. You had my Allison and armor picked up and brought along. I figure that means something."

"Less than you think," said Li-hon.

"I just want to know what to expect."

"Expect the worst," Mlas said in a clipped tone. "That way you're never surprised. And picking up bodies is about as bad as it comes. I'd rather wrestle a Warri." He pushed back from the battle board and stood. "Permission to withdraw, sergeant? I'll pass the word to my people."

"Granted. Any more questions?" Li-hon asked, his gaze sweeping around the circle. "If not, get. I don't want to see any of you until Captain Yier sounds the entry alarm tomorrow afternoon."

Twenty minutes after the alarm sounded, the members of the Ninth came together on *Zephyr's* bridge to look on as the ship entered the six-planet Cavalon system.

The two outermost worlds were cold, pale-colored hydrogen-helium balls. *Zephyr's* trajectory took it within two light-minutes of the outermost, designated Wegn—six—in the standard numbering system. Tracked by the ship's long-range viewers, Wegn slipped by to starboard like some gaseous ghost in the eternal night.

Ahead lay four small terrestrial worlds clustered close to the orange dwarf star itself. To Bhodi's surprise, their destination was Ehl, the closest in. He had thought that, like Mercury in his home system, Ehl would be too fiercely hot to accommodate life.

But all Ehl needed to become more hospitable was an improvement on its thin, oxygen- and water-poor atmosphere. So Ehl's crystal had been programmed to create an atmosphere that would screen Cavalon's harshest rays and restore the geochemical cycles which had been interrupted long ago.

"Cavalon went through an active period about 1.8 billion years ago," Parcival told Bhodi. "It boiled off most of the lighter gases and virtually all of the surface water. This was a really promising place for life at one time."

"It isn't now," Bhodi said, studying the even more detailed image appearing on the forward window. Ehl was brown and desolate, its face pockmarked and creased, a forbidding world.

"Sensors are picking up no sign of the courier in orbit," Captain Yier reported.

That news seemed to trouble Li-hon. "Have you begun surface scans?"

"Forty percent complete. No sign—wait. High reflectance anomaly on the surface. Coordinates fifteen-mark-six lateral, twenty-eight–mark-two polar."

"*I'olhlm*," Pike said.

"Maybe," said Li-hon.

"Getting some residual Photon radiation now off the same site," one of the other crewmen announced. "Forty-six—fifty—fifty-four count. Confirming, profile matches a leaking fractional drive power unit."

"What mass?" asked Parcival.

"Uh—looks like a four-mass."

Parcival turned to Li-hon. "Then that's not *I'olhlm*. That has to be the *Majestic*." But there was puzzlement in his voice, not the excitement of discovery. "What's she doing on the surface? Couriers aren't dustbellies."

"You've got two choices," Pike observed. "Either they crashed, or they crash-landed."

No one wanted to choose an answer. But as they fell into orbit above the spot where the anomaly rested, the high-res scanners picked out a triangular silver hull resting half in the shadow of a granite cliff.

"I thought for sure it'd be scattered in little pieces across the landscape," Pike said, shaking his head. "She looks like she's in pretty good shape, considering. Maybe we're dealing with an accident after all.''

"Maybe." Li-hon addressed Parcival, who was peering over the shoulder of the ship's sensor technician. "Can we pop down to her, or do we have to fly?"

"I'm not picking up any recognition code from *Majestic's* transporter."

"Are you getting *anything* coherent?"

"No. She's radio-dead."

"Okay." He turned to Captain Yier. "I'm going to take the platoon down in landing pod A. I want Mlas and six of his Regulars standing by in B with full medpacks, ready to come down as soon as we give the all-clear."

Then he turned back to the others. "Full battle gear, everyone. Atmosphere's not much to chew on down there—Parcival, Bhodi, you'll need the bubbles. Pike, you can get by with a breather. Move! I want you in the pod in five minutes. There may be people hurting down there."

Ehl was even more forbidding up close than from orbit—a desolate landscape of weathered scarps and granite block mountains linked by desertlike expanses. The wind was blowing constantly, but the air was so thin that it could do little more than kick up dust devils and whistle in the bubble helmet's external microphones.

The surroundings made the wreck of the *Majestic* look even more forlorn and forsaken than it otherwise would have. Its presence was of no consequence whatsoever to the planet, like a burr on the shaggy coat of a golden retriever. The courier's descent and death had gone completely unnoticed.

As the pod descended toward the fault valley in which the hulk rested, Bhodi and the other passengers could see that *Majestic* must have come in at low speed and reason-

ably under control. The great hull rested tail-high and
tipped to starboard, both angles dictated by the irregular
shape of the ship's underbelly and which parts of the
superstructure had collapsed under the unusual stress.

Li-hon landed the cylindrical pod a cautious 200 meters
away from the ship. Then he turned to Parcival and asked,
"Any activity out there?"

Parcival consulted the pod's sensors, then his own wrist-
mounted black box. "Nothing showing."

"Okay. Bhodi, stay with the pod—"

"But—" Bhodi cut off his own protest. He had nothing
to gain by jerking at the traces.

Li-hon seemed not to notice Bhodi had spoken at all.
"Parcival, set up an alarm on the sensors on Bhodi's
frequency. I want him outside as a sentry, not locked up in
here staring at dials and gauges."

"Done," said Parcival.

Bhodi came outside with them and stood watching as
they started toward the massive spaceship. The sight reminded Bhodi of a photo in his freshman science text. The
photo had showed a freighter resting high and dry in a
field after being pushed ashore by a tsunami—a jarring
clash of context.

Then duty called, and he began walking his beat—a
slow circuit of the pod, scanning the surrounding walls of
rock. While he walked, he eavesdropped on the radio
traffic. There were three circuits in the battlefield com
loop: a general-use circuit called the omni, a receiver-
selectable circuit called the whisper, and Li-hon's priority-
override command circuit. Most of the traffic was on the
omni.

"A hell of a job of piloting."

"The D section's all caved in—I hope everybody was
out of those cabins."

"I don't see any reason yet why the core pressure hull can't be intact."

"Look—underneath, around the port cylinder intake. She burned, at least for a while."

"Probably on impact—"

They were near enough to *Majestic* to be lost in her shadow when Parcival called out, "Is that a body?"

"Sure is—sweet Light, the poor thing's all torn up. Didn't they have enough sense to brace and strap in?"

"Bhodi?" It was Li-hon, on the command circuit.

"Yes, sir," Bhodi said eagerly.

"Anything on the activity board?"

"Just you three."

"All right. The external recon shows crash damage, scorching, one casualty. The site looks clean, but we're going to go slow. I'm posting Parcival outside here. Pike and I are going inside to check the crystal vault and look for other bodies. Call up to Captain Yier and tell him to send the Regulars down."

Bhodi did as he was asked, disappointed that he was not being asked to do more. When Captain Yier signed off, Bhodi switched from the omni to whisper mode. "Parcival?"

"What's up?"

"Any sign yet what brought the ship down?"

"Nothing obvious."

"She wasn't shot down?"

"If she had been, she'd be in a lot more pieces."

"What do you think happened?"

"Well—couriers aren't dustbellies, like I said. But neither are the Arr galleons. Captain Lasdree must have been trying to run to the only place he thought he had a chance of saving either the crystals or his people."

"Any sign he managed either?"

"Not yet. Look, I'm going to do a walkaround. Can you watch the front door from there?"

"Sure."

Switching back to the omni circuit, Bhodi watched as Parcival's diminutive form disappeared around the rear quarter of the ship. A minute passed.

"Sergeant!" Parcival shouted suddenly.

"Yes, Parcival."

"I've got a faint life reading in there. Looks like we've got at least one survivor."

"All right. We're getting close to the vault. We'll finish that and then try to track down that life reading. Bhodi?"

"Still all clear."

"Keep your eyes open. Don't rely on the sensors completely."

"Understood."

For almost two minutes—an infinity of time under the circumstances—the radio was silent. Bhodi caught an occasional glimpse of Parcival picking his way along under the belly of the courier, but other than that Bhodi might have been alone on the barren, windswept valley floor.

"We're at the vault," Li-hon said finally. "It's closed and intact. Opening her up now."

"Wait a minute," Parcival said, his voice quavery.

"What?"

"I'm looking at the other side. All this damage wasn't done in the crash. These holes are burned from the outside in. Half a sec—sergeant, there's something odd about that life reading—"

Almost without thinking, Bhodi began to take tentative steps in the direction of the wreck. Then from Pike came a frantic cry: "Look out!"

Bhodi did not wait to hear more. He took off at a run toward *Majestic*, his Allison in hand, the pod open and undefended behind him. The sound of phaser fire reached him faintly through the helmet mikes. Then came the words that chilled him like ice pressed to the middle of his back.

"Bhodi!" Li-hon cried. "Full alert! The ship's dirty! The vault's full of Dogs!"

CHAPTER 18

With a mouth large enough to engulf a human head, jaws strong enough to snap a femur like a matchstick, and a spiked tail that would have been at home on a stegosaurus, a Dog was never a welcome sight. To have one spring at you without warning out of the darkness, snarling and clawing, was almost too much to bear.

Only the speed of Pike's reflexes prevented the surprise from being a fatal one. He had been standing a step behind and just to the right of Li-hon as the sergeant made the sign of the Light and entered the Guard's special override code into the vault controller. When the door began to slide open, Pike was the first to glimpse movement inside the vault.

The possibility that some of *Majestic's* complement had taken refuge in the vault kept Pike from firing blindly through the gap between the moving door and the jamb. But he was on alert, and when the stale-cooking-grease smell of Dog reached the olfactory sensors in the roof of his mouth, his fingers squeezed down on the trigger of his Allison without conscious thought.

As the first Dog lunged through the doorway, Li-hon started backpedaling in search of fighting room, barking out a warning to the rest of the platoon. His scope-sighted pulse cannon was slung on his back, out of reach but useless anyway in close quarters.

With a clear target at last, Pike fired into the Dog's gaping mouth, and a smell like burnt cinnamon flooded the room. The Dog screamed, shook its head violently, and prepared to launch itself at Pike. But Pike's next shot seared the Dog's eyes, unprotected under the rim of the ornate helmet. Its snarl turned into a squeal of pain, and the creature shied and rocked back on its tail, clawing at its face.

But by then a second Dog had burst through the opening and past Pike in pursuit of Li-hon. Pike finished off the first Dog with a long shot that burned down through its flat forehead and into its braincase, then he turned to see what he could do for his commander.

Vibrablade gripped in his right hand, Li-hon had stopped his retreat and was keeping the Dog at bay with powerful kicks from his booted right foot. But instead of ducking or flinching from the kicks, the Dog was perversely turning its head towards each blow, enduring the battering for a chance to snap at—and maybe snap off—Li-hon's foot.

So far Li-hon had been quicker, but his sledgehammer blows did not seem to be having any effect. The close calls with the Dog's jaws had already left deep gouges in the thick boot material, and the surface of the boot was coated with the Dog's acidic saliva.

Pike targeted the sensitive area near the base of the Arrian's tail and squeezed the trigger. It was not a potentially killing shot, but he expected the Dog to turn on him, giving Li-hon a chance to use the blade.

But instead, the Dog yelped and lunged forward toward the enemy in its eyes, seizing Li-hon's left leg above the knee and tearing away a dinner-plate-sized swatch of the reinforced fighting suit and a huge gobbet of the leathery flesh underneath.

The vibrablade came down and carved a canyon through the Dog's massive neck, and the beast's legs buckled. It fell slack-jawed at Li-hon's feet, the end of its tail twitching three times before the light in its black eyes died. Blood was everywhere, both the thick deep cherry-red variety coursing from Li-hon's wound and the Dog's thin ocher slime.

Li-hon rocked back on his heels, the tension draining from his limbs. He slipped the vibrablade into the half-shredded sheath on his left boot and looked toward Pike.

"Stupid, stupid, stupid," he said. "I always feel like I'm trespassing when I go into a vault without a crystal handler there. I never stopped to think that an Arrian might actually consider hiding inside. As if they would respect the place and what it means. Stupid."

"Don't kick yourself too hard. It's a new trick," Pike said. "Almost more creative than I thought they were capable of. You all right?"

Li-hon glanced down at his thigh. The concave wound was deep, raw and ugly, but the thick blood was already congealing into a rubbery jelly. "For now," he said. "Let's finish this."

They picked their way past the bodies of their attackers and into the vault. There were eight crystal receptacles in the arch-ceilinged chamber, four on each side. Li-hon was not surprised to see that they were all empty, the locking bars burned through and bent back by brute force.

"They got the crystals," Li-hon announced tautly on the command circuit. "Bhodi? Parcival? Report. What's going on out there?"

Bhodi and Parcival had their own problems. Li-hon's alert had brought Bhodi running, but also brought Parcival scampering back around to the near side of *Majestic* and the entry point the others had used. The moment Parcival saw Bhodi coming across the valley floor, he went wild.

"Get back to your post!" Parcival screamed. "Get back to your post!"

Uncertainty prompted by Parcival's words caused Bhodi to slow his steps. Just as he did, a high-powered phaser blast blackened the sand just in front of him, exactly where he would have been had he kept stride.

He stumbled into a dive roll and came up running once more. Since he was more than halfway to *Majestic,* he kept going in that direction, zigzagging as sharply as the footing would allow. His chest was tight with terror. His skin prickled with anticipation of the fiery heat that would take his legs out from under him and drop him in the open to die. Ahead, Parcival ducked into the shelter of *Majestic's* hatchway.

But it did not seem as though Bhodi were fired at again. When he joined Parcival in the hatchway, Bhodi could finally afford to look back and see why. The gunner had turned his attention to the pod, and with devastating effect, showing the power of the weapon he was using. There were two scorched holes in the hull already, and a flickering light inside showed that the pod was starting to burn.

"You were saying?" Bhodi said tersely.

Parcival ignored him. "I notified Captain Yier that we've got snipers and had him recall the Regulars. No sense bringing them down into the middle of this."

Bhodi peeked out the doorway again. "Awfully considerate, considering you didn't even bother to give me any covering fire. They're right up there on that high ridge, along the south rim—"

"Forget it. We can't do anything from here except get ourselves in more trouble," Parcival said. "Which is why you didn't get any cover fire."

"Why can't we do anything?"

"Too far." He glanced at his right wrist, checking the rangemeter. "They're 430 meters away."

"I can hit them—"

"But you can't hurt them. Inverse-square rule—distance costs power. You can't light up the new moon with a flashlight. And phasers are nothing but fancy flashlights."

With a *whump* that echoed off the rock faces of the valley, what was left of the pod exploded. Fragments large and small scattered in a circle around it.

"Then we'll have to go up and get them," Bhodi said.

"How? Charge the ridge? Face facts, Bhodi. We're outgunned. Let's be glad *Majestic's* got a thick skin and go see if we can help the Sarge."

That was when both heard the welcome sound of Li-hon's voice demanding their report. Parcival quickly summarized the situation for Li-hon, courteously leaving out any mention of Bhodi abandoning his post.

"Stay put," Li-hon said. "We'll be there in a moment."

Four made a crowd in the entryway. Li-hon took the spot nearest the open hatch, with Parcival pressed into a corner beside him. Pike filled the middle of the chamber, and Bhodi found himself pushed nearly out of the compartment and completely out of the conversation.

"How many do you think?" Li-hon asked Parcival.

"There's only a single fire point. I'd say one, with a C-class laser cannon."

"Another Dog?" Pike wondered.

"No," Li-hon said. "They don't have the discipline to work as snipers. A Dog would've come charging down out of the rocks the minute we stepped out of the pod."

"A Destructor, then."

"That's my guess," Parcival said.

Li-hon nodded. "He's there to pick off anyone that gets

away from the Dogs. Except he should have left the pod alone, so we'd have a reason to come out. Not too smart.''

"Like I said, a Destructor," Pike said with a crooked grin. "What do you say?''

"Whatever we do, we have to do fast.''

"Why?'' Bhodi said from the rear.

Li-hon twisted his head to look back at Bhodi. "Because the Arrians can't support a nest this deep in our territory, and they wouldn't just abandon a team here, even for a clever ambush.''

Bhodi suddenly understood. "Which means that there's an Arr ship somewhere upstairs playing hide and seek with *Zephyr* and a warren somewhere down here with the crystals inside.''

"Exactly so. And if we want to get them back and save this planet for the Light, we've got to get moving.''

"Not to mention if we want to get out of this valley alive.''

"That, too.''

Pike edged forward to steal a peek out the door. "Quiet out there now. Do you have the spot?''

"Yes,'' Li-hon said. "If he hasn't moved.''

"I'll bet he is moving. He's got his choice of a thousand meters of ridge.''

"Ideas, anyone?'' Li-hon asked.

Pike shook his head. "There isn't going to be much we can do if our friend keeps his head down. Gonna be hard to get above him. What about a little air support? Let Mlas bring the other pod down and have a shot at him.''

"No,'' Li-hon said. "He may have friends elsewhere in the rocks. We can't risk the second pod.''

Bhodi suggested, "What about the chances of cutting the cliff out from under his feet? Parcival?''

"I was thinking about that myself and ran a couple

quick calculations. That's solid granite. I don't think we could cut it faster than he could move."

Pike looked to Li-hon and eyed the pair of club-handled grenades tucked into the Qeth's utility belt. "Think you can reach the top with a tin can?"

"If I have time to get out the door and get my feet planted solidly, and if we can keep him from burning it on the way down."

"And if we know where he is."

"I'll draw," Parcival said, edging toward the door.

"I'll cover," Pike said. "Give me the pipe."

Li-hon unsnapped the sling on the pulse cannon and passed it to Pike.

"What do you want me to do?" Bhodi asked.

"Stay put."

"No," Bhodi said. "Not again. I'll draw. Not Parcival."

"Don't treat me like a kid, Bhodi," Parcival said. "It's my job."

"It's not that," Bhodi said, shaking his head. "I'm faster than you are, so I've got a better chance of not getting hit. And I'm less valuable than you, so if I do get hit, it doesn't matter."

Parcival looked to Li-hon, asking for his adjudication.

"Right on both counts," Li-hon pronounced. "Come up here, Bhodi. You're first out the door."

Bhodi did not quite understand why he had volunteered to offer himself as a target to the Arrian gunner high in the rocks. But as he crouched in the doorway, tensing in anticipation of Li-hon's signal, he knew that it was the right thing to do.

It was more than rebellion against being sheltered from danger, more than his inability to forget that Parcival was the same age as Ralphie-next-door, who still cried over skinned knees. It was more even than pride and ego driving him to show that he wasn't afraid.

It was, he thought, linked somehow to the sudden insight that, in this moment at least, the platoon was better with him than without him—that with his contribution, more of them might make it back to *Zephyr*, even if he himself did not.

That seemed to be the reason, but it did not make sense. He owed them nothing, least of all his own life. He hadn't accepted their fight as his own, hadn't acknowledged any responsibility for anyone's survival but his own. But here he was, about to tempt fate twice, and perversely happy about it.

He locked his gaze on the burned-out shell of the pod. *If I can reach there, I'll have cover*, he told himself. *What's the world record time for 200 meters? Twenty seconds? I could sure hit me with that much time—*

Li-hon touched Bhodi's shoulder. "We're ready. Remember—evasive. You can't outrun a phaser bolt."

"Fine last words for me to hear," Bhodi said and leaped out onto the sand.

There was no place for Parcival in the queue that was forming at the door, so he maneuvered himself into a place where he and the combat recorder built into the chest pod would have a clear view of the action.

Bhodi was the first out, lighting down smoothly and sprinting toward the pod. His long strides ate up the open ground quickly—ten meters, twenty, thirty. Parcival caught himself whispering under his breath: *Run, Bhodi, run like you never have*.

Then the Arrian sniper opened up, and things started happening. Bhodi ran through the fringe of the sniper's ranging shot, stumbled and broke stride. Parcival feared for a moment that Bhodi was going to fall down, which would almost certainly be fatal. But he caught himself and angled sharply right, limping slightly.

An eye blink later, Li-hon jumped down to the ground, his gaze locked on the sniper's new location. After a two-step windup that reminded Parcival of an outfielder cranking up for a throw from right field to home, Li-hon let fly with the grenade in his right hand.

At the same time, Pike stood up in the entryway and opened fire, raking the cliff's edge with the pulse cannon. His efforts created a cascade of rock litter down the near-vertical slope and drew the sniper's attention away from Bhodi.

The grenade arched high in the air, propelled by Li-hon's muscular explosion. But either his estimate of the distance was wrong or his injured left leg did not give him the thrust he needed. The grenade bounced harmlessly against the granite wall a bare meter or two from the top, skittered down the face, and exploded harmlessly in mid-air.

Head turned to the side as he ran, Bhodi saw the gre-nade fall short, and Parcival could almost feel Bhodi's anxiety surge to new heights in the instant following. His gait noticeably slowed by the hit he had taken, Bhodi lowered his head and cut back to the left.

But Bhodi was no longer the most important target for the Arrian. Following typical Destructor priorities, the sniper fixed his attention on the largest "enemy" at hand. *Majestic's* hull sizzled as the sniper poured energy onto it. Pike answered back shot for shot, trying to force the sniper to cover.

Li-hon stood calmly in the open, seemingly oblivious to the thousands of watts of energy pouring down in his direction from the cliff. He armed the second grenade, took it in his left hand this time, and hurled it toward the rocks with a Herculean effort. His left leg buckled and he went to one knee to watch the flight of the clublike bomb, making no effort to retreat into the wreck.

Higher, higher, the grenade flew, spinning gracefully end for end, until it reached the apogee of its arc and started downward. Too late the sniper saw it, and redirected his fire upward. But the phaser cannon was a poor weapon against a small, fast-moving object, and the grenade fell untouched on the high plateau just a few meters to the east of the sniper's position.

An instant later that entire section of the cliff's edge lit up with an eerie light like a massive lightning strike, and a sound like thunder rumbled through the valley. Lowering the pulse cannon from his shoulder, Pike slipped down from the entryway and went to Li-hon's side. A hundred meters away on the valley floor, Bhodi came to a stop and started walking back.

"What the hell was that?" Pike asked.

"An enhanced-yield grenade," Parcival said, coming forward out of the ship. "I've been working on them for the Sarge."

"Correction," Li-hon said. "That was the end of one sniper." He reached for his chest pod and signaled the ship. "Captain Yier. Send the pod down, all possible speed. The Regulars have a lot of work to do down here, and we've got an Arrian warren to find."

It was all over, and yet not quite. Bhodi found himself waiting for someone to recognize him for what he had done, for Li-hon to amend his estimation of Bhodi's worth to the platoon.

But beyond asking about Bhodi's condition—a hamstring had suddenly tightened up when he stutter-stepped at full speed—Li-hon said nothing to Bhodi while they waited for the pod's arrival. Bhodi was not sure what he expected or even deserved—do you thank someone for doing their job? Or their duty?

But a short time later, as they left the pod after docking with *Zephyr*, Bhodi overheard a brief exchange between Yier and Li-hon that gave him everything that he could have asked for.

"How did the kid do?" Yier asked.

"I didn't bring any kids with me," Li-hon said as he brushed by. "But Bhodi did all right."

CHAPTER 19

It took three hours and two orbits to locate the Arrian warren. The entrance was at the center of a small crater in a lightly cratered, boulder-strewn plain—well-disguised, except that the freshness of the diggings showed on one of Parcival's instruments.

"The warren can't be very extensive," Li-hon said, leaning forward over the battle board and its projection of the cratered plain. "They've been here at most five days. I'd expect three or four chambers at most. But that means that they'll be sitting right inside. We'll pay for every corner and foot of passageway."

He glanced up at Bhodi. "I have to tell you that this isn't what I thought we'd find here. I expected the Arrians and the crystals both to be gone, and all you'd have to deal with would be bodies and wrecks. But the Arrians and the crystals are here, and we have to go after them. You don't."

"Are you saying you don't want me as your partner?"

"I'm saying I've got no authority to order you to go down with us. Not when your finger is still bare. You can stay with the ship—"

"No way," Bhodi said. "You've got all the authority

193

you need, from me. You tell me what has to be done, and I'll try my damnedest to get it done.''

"No one will judge you if you stay. I have to know that you understand that.''

"Yes, they will. And even if they didn't, I would,'' Bhodi said. "Come on, we're wasting time. How are we going to do this?''

Li-hon looked hard into Bhodi's eyes as though trying to take the measure of his soul through them. "Thank you,'' he said at last. "Frankly, we're shorthanded for a warren assault. I wish I had the whole platoon and another squad of Regulars. But we don't have them, and the Arrians will be gone and this planet contaminated before reinforcements could get here. So we'll do what we can with what we have, and with the blessing of the Light we'll take our enemies down.''

"By the Light,'' Pike murmured in agreement.

Crossing his arms over his chest, Li-hon stared down at the battle board. "They haven't had any time to build any decoys, so we have to respect the possibility they'll take a shot at the pod on the way down. Corporal Mlas—''

"You know I'll take you in as close as you want,'' Mlas said. "I'll drop you in the crater itself if you ask me.''

"I think the closest we can risk is somewhere in here,'' Li-hon said, drawing an arc over a boulder-free region east of the warren with the tip of his finger.

Pike frowned. "It'll take a while to get to them from there. How much time do you think we have?''

"They've already surprised us twice, once by striking here, and again with the ambush. At the risk of being surprised again, I'd say that we have until their ship appears, plus maybe an hour.''

Nodding, Parcival said to Bhodi in an aside, "They don't put much of a delay on the timer. Once the Dark Terror starts moving in for the pickup, you know that the clock is running.''

"Maybe we can surprise them ourselves," Pike said thoughtfully.

"How?" Bhodi asked. "They already know we're here."

"Right. So we don't lose anything if we move *Zephyr* right overhead. Let them think they know where we are and wonder when we're coming down after them. While they're wondering, we'll be coming in on the deck in the pod."

"Because we separated on the other side of the planet."

"Right. Hopefully they'll be so busy watching *Zephyr* that we'll be able to get down without any interference, and maybe a lot closer than the Sarge thinks." He grinned crookedly. "You know how I hate to walk."

Ten minutes later they were on their way down. Jikt of the ship's crew piloted the crowded pod, which carried six Regulars in addition to Bhodi and the three Guardians.

Either Jikt's reflexes or the terrain-hugging radar was superb. The pod pitched and dove so violently as it followed the contours of the ground that Bhodi had to turn his head away from the forward view to keep from becoming nauseous.

At no time were they ever more than twenty feet above the surface, and Bhodi swore that they were clearing some of the outcrops of rock by mere inches. Finally they came down out of the foothills and skimmed over the boulder field, remnant of a glacial epoch long ago in Ehl's history.

As they closed on the target, Jikt sang out the range: "Two thousand meters. Eighteen hundred. Sixteen hundred—"

"Don't you wish sometimes you could just bomb the hell out of them and bury them in their caves?" Bhodi asked Parcival on the whisper link.

"Every time," was the answer.

As they approached the 1200-meter circle, a jarring

alarm started to sound inside the pod. "Somebody just pitched a rocket at us," Jikt called out.

"Perimeter guard," Li-hon said tersely. "Put us down here."

"Roger. Hold on."

The sudden deceleration threw Bhodi forward against the restraining straps, and he fought his stomach as the pod pitched downward sharply. A few moments later they were on the ground. As Bhodi tore at the strap catches, a muffled explosion nearby made the pod vibrate.

"I think we went right over top of them. Too fast for them to take a bead. They just tossed up a prayer," Jikt said, craning his head and listening.

"Range to target?"

"Eight hundred thirty meters," Parcival announced.

"Too close to leave the pod here," Li-hon said, standing in the crowded cabin. "Jikt, take it back out the way you came in and put it down at the site on the 3000-meter circle."

"Shall I assign sentries to stay with the pod?" Corporal Mlas asked.

"No," Li-hon said. "We can't afford to surrender twenty percent of our strength in the name of standard practice. Sorry, Jikt."

"I'll be all right," the pilot said easily.

Li-hon nodded. "Let's move, people. Everybody out."

The terrain where Jikt had set them down was less rugged than some they had flown over. There was a slight uphill slope in the direction of the crater. Fewer boulders were in evidence, and those that were present were more deeply buried. All of those features were courtesy of the meteorite that had created the crater, splashing the material that had filled it onto the surrounding plain.

As the pod roared away, Li-hon began dividing his

meager forces, delegating Pike to lead Parcival and two of the Regulars, Mlas among them, to hunt down the Arrian perimeter sentries. "I don't want any nasties coming up behind us while we approach the warren," he said.

"You figure we're dealing with Dogs?"

"They're the Arrian rocket specialists," Li-hon said. "At least they always have been. I'm beginning to think I don't know anything about the Arrians. When have they ever posted perimeter guards around an untouched warren?"

Pike bobbed his head. "This whole raid—the ambush, the perimeter guard—all out of character. The Warri captains have been so predictable. You don't think that maybe Mandarr—"

"I do—but I don't want to."

"I thought Intelligence put him in Dray Sector."

"So did I," said Li-hon. "They may have been wrong."

Pike made a clucking noise. "We'll protect your back. Go root 'em out. Patrol—three abreast, space to sight. I'll take the point." He turned and strode westward, in the direction of the explosion. Parcival and the two Regulars fanned out and followed.

"Who's Mandarr?" Bhodi asked as the remaining combatants closed in around Li-hon.

Li-hon frowned. "A new Arrian commander. The Warlord seems to have given him a freer hand than his other commanders. All this might be his doing." He waved the Regulars forward. "Let's move. We've got work to do. We'll use a pairs line, space fifty. You, you, right flank," he said pointing. "You two, left flank. Bhodi Li and I will take the center. Free-fire rules. And let's keep the chatter on the omni to a minimum, all right? The enemy does like to listen in."

They picked their way toward the crater cautiously and in silence, guns drawn, eyes alert. As they paused in the cover of a half-buried boulder for the flank pairs to catch up, Li-hon watched Bhodi closely.

The youth seemed calm, but that was no reassurance. Better he should let himself feel his fear and use the adrenaline that came with it than to deny it and suppress it until it built to where it overwhelmed him.

"Sergeant." It was Pike on the whisper circuit.

"Here, Pike."

"It gets curiouser and curiouser. We've got us a Dog here, armed with a rocket launcher—"

"Just as we thought."

"—running from us."

"Repeat?"

"I said we've got a well-armed, uninjured Dog running from us. Who are these guys?"

"Are you sure he knows you're there?"

"I toasted his tail not two minutes ago. He knows."

The corners of Li-hon's mouth wrinkled with puzzlement. "Well—it makes sense, actually. The rocket launcher's a lousy weapon for one-on-one. And he's got no hands to pull it off and mount a phaser. He's got to go find a Warri."

"Sure, it makes sense," Pike retorted. "But when did a Dog ever do the sensible thing in combat? They just like to rip and burn."

"What do you think, then?"

"I think he's trying to draw us away from something."

"What kind of something?"

"Don't know. Permission to let him go and look around?"

"I don't want to lose track of the Dog," Li-hon said. "Send Mlas to shadow him. Then give a quick look-see. But remember, there's probably more than one sentry out there, and they'll be coming your way."

"Let 'em come," Pike said. "It'll be a reassuring sight. Dogs running from a fight—this is getting too weird."

• • •

The lip of the crater was in sight when the assault force got the bad news from *Zephyr*.

"We're going to have company up here," Captain Yier announced. "An Arr ship just popped on the scopes. She must have been orbiting Neph in lights-out mode, or maybe sitting on the surface. Anyway, she's got it lit up now. You've got about twenty minutes before she gets within transporter range, maybe less."

"I thought—" Bhodi began.

"Later," Li-hon said sharply. "Captain Yier, we've got to have more time. You'll have to engage and try to hold her off."

"I don't think she's going to want to play," Yier said. "But I'll get you what I can."

Li-hon turned to Bhodi. "Now, what?"

"Nothing. It's just that I thought the transporter could throw you all the way across a stellar system."

"The Arrian transporter is different than ours," Li-hon said, turning his attention back to the crater ahead. "Shorter range, but one big advantage: They can grab their people back from the surface without a focus grid at this end."

"Not from inside the warren?"

"No. Not through all that dirt and rock."

"So in the middle of fighting our way in, we might find them trying to fight their way out. And then they could just vanish on us?"

"Yep," Li-hon said grimly. "And if it happens, you start running the other way—because you don't want to be in the neighborhood when an Arrian crystal is set off. B'ere'a, Kree-tih, are you set?"

The answers came back from both flanks in the affirmative.

Li-hon looked to Bhodi. "Then let's go."

They reached the rim of the crater without incident.

When they looked down over the edge, the crater was deserted. There was no doubt of that, since there was no place in the great earthen bowl to hide.

Bhodi thought briefly that he would hate to come under fire on the crater floor, then pushed the thought away as he focused on the three mounds and their black maws. *Which one?* he wondered. *A lady and two tigers. Which one's the lady?*

With silent hand signals, Li-hon called one Regular from each flank up to the rim of the crater. Quietly and efficiently, they took up positions 180 degrees apart and 90 degrees from where Li-hon and Bhodi lay—perfect for covering fire.

Digging the pockets of his belt, Li-hon came up with a pair of handball-sized metal spheres. "You take the entry on the near left," Li-hon said, handing one of the squealers to Bhodi. Invaluable for warren-cracking, the squealers simulated the sounds of a Guardian moving in one of the passageways, triggering some types of booby traps and occasionally drawing an incautious Warri out of hiding. "Remember, just roll it down the chute."

"Got it," Bhodi said. He checked the readouts of his Allison one last time, then took a deep breath and went over the top.

The crater was about three meters deep, and the wall was steep and crumbly. Bhodi dropped to the crater floor in a controlled slide, his eyes scanning the shadowed entrances. There was no movement, no phasers winking in his direction.

Bhodi started across the crater floor in a crouch. From behind came the sounds of Li-hon following him down the slope. Bhodi was aware of Li-hon, of the Regulars perched on the rim, ready to burn any Arrian who suddenly popped up from a warren entrance—but suddenly the fear sweat was running down the middle of his back.

Suddenly he could not take one more step, could not face what was waiting down under the surface of this dead world. He wanted to throw the Allison as far away as he could and cry, "Don't kill me, I don't belong here, this isn't my fight!"

Then someone screamed in pain, and for a confused moment Bhodi thought it was him. A moment later he realized that the sound had come over the omni circuit. He twisted around to face the way he had come, looking for explanations. He saw only Li-hon, equally puzzled.

"Something got B'ere'a," Kree-tih shouted. "On the west rim—"

Li-hon looked up and started to swing his pulse cannon in that direction. "Run, Bhodi!" he cried.

But Bhodi froze, horrified, as he watched Li-hon suddenly savaged by a flurry of phaser blasts. The first turned the fingers of Li-hon's right hand, wrapped around the forward grip of the cannon, into smoking stubs too short to maintain their hold. As the weapon fell from his shoulder to the crater floor, another hit seared the right side of Li-hon face, the skin bubbling up into blisterlike cysts.

At last Li-hon started to move, turning away and unleashing a guttural bellow that had to mean an agony Bhodi could only imagine. The movement made a shot aimed at Li-hon's chest pod miss and burn deep into his side instead. Li-hon took one step, wobbled, and went down. And still the enemy kept firing, tracing a line from the base of Li-hon's tail up across his shoulders.

And the reality of it all suddenly came home to Bhodi in a way that no amount of training, not even the skirmish at *Majestic,* had managed to bring home. He was watching Li-hon—his friend and commander Nar-lex-ko-li-hon—die. And something deep and fundamental inside Bhodi rebelled and took command of him.

"No!" Bhodi shouted.

Sometimes the choice is charge the enemy or die—

Bhodi charged, and from behind Kree-tih tried vainly to protect him. In the first five steps, Bhodi took a hit in the chest armor, then another in the faceplate, nearly blinding him. He fired back wildly, his pounding strides making aim impossible. Halfway up the crater wall, his left leg tightened up again. He would not let it slow him. Clawing, crawling, he scrambled upward to the rim of the crater and threw himself over the edge. He landed on a body— B'ere'a—rolled over once and came to his knees, seeking a target for his Allison.

The target was there, crouching less than five paces away. But Bhodi froze, unable to pull the trigger. For the enemy was not one he was prepared for. It was not Warri or Bug, not Dog or Destructor. Behind the enemy's helmet visor Bhodi glimpsed a human face.

Or nearly human. The eyes gazed outward through black metal eyeshields that seemed to have been surgically inserted, and the left temple and cheek bore a pattern of silver tracings like computer wiring. Bhodi stared unbelievingly as the warrior, as though sensing Bhodi's paralysis, slowly rose to his full height.

Then came the second shock, greater by far than the first. "Too reckless," the man-machine said, and Bhodi knew the voice. "You were always too reckless."

And he raised his right hand, the hand holding the massive phaser pistol, as Bhodi tried to deny what could not be denied: that this was Mandarr, the unpredictable, the new lieutenant of the Warlord of Arr. And that Mandarr was—or once had been—Bhodi's friend, Evan Kyley.

CHAPTER 20

Bhodi should have been dead, and he knew it.

But even looking down the barrel of Mandarr's high-powered weapon and realizing that in the next second it could release a torrent of energy to steal his life away, Bhodi could not make his finger close on the firing contact of the Allison. There were too many unanswered questions embodied in Kyley's presence and appearance. Bhodi could not strike him down without finding answers. Why Mandarr was hesitating, Bhodi did not know.

With the clarity that came with a cusp moment, Bhodi took in a thousand details in one glance. Kyley-Mandarr seemed to be wired into his accordion-pleated fighting suit. It was festooned with power jumpers, what looked like hydraulic lines, and tiny spiderlike electronic boxes with silver leads. Yet for just a moment, Bhodi could strip all that away and remember facing off with Kyley with infrared pistols for $3.50 a match.

It was Kree-tih and his partner that saved Bhodi, bracketing Mandarr with a crossfire that did no damage but did distract the Arrian for an instant. In that instant Bhodi dove at Mandarr, spearing him in the midsection with the crown of his helmet. As they toppled over together, Bhodi clawed for the jumper that fed Mandarr's weapon from his power belt and tore it loose.

Just as quickly, the advantage swung back the other way. With a swipe of his right arm, Mandarr knocked Bhodi off to one side. The blow would have broken Bhodi's neck had it not been for his helmet, and jarred him badly despite it. Kyley had always been stronger than Christopher Jarvis; the gap between Mandarr and Bhodi Li seemed even wider.

Rolling to hands and knees, Bhodi looked up just in time to throw his left arm in the way of a left-handed punch. At least it seemed like a punch, until Bhodi felt something stab deep into the meat of his forearm and then the sticky warmth of blood flowing inside his fighting suit.

As Mandarr jerked his hand back, Bhodi saw what Mandarr's raw strength had driven through both the armor and the suit. Strapped to the Arrian's wrist was a multi-bladed cutter with razor-sharp edges and toothlike spurs. Mandarr slashed out with it once more, a sweeping roundhouse lunge in the direction of Bhodi's chest. Bhodi leaped back, stumbled, and went to one knee.

Instead of pursuing the advantage, Mandarr took that moment to try to reattach his phaser's power jumper, which had come free at the connector instead of breaking in half. It was an almost contemptuous move on Mandarr's part, as though he was so certain of his superiority that he need not worry about granting Bhodi a short reprieve.

But the throbbing pain in Bhodi's forearm and the blood collecting in his left gauntlet had erased any reservations he had about fighting to win. Whipping his Allison up to eye level, Bhodi blasted Mandarr's faceplate until it charcoaled into permanent opacity.

"What's happening, Evan?" he screamed. "What are you doing here?"

With a sweeping motion of his left hand, Mandarr tore

his helmet off and flung it to one side. Bhodi gasped, then gaped. Most of the right side of Kyley's skull had been shaved to make room for the silver wire leads and the tiny computer box above his ear to which they were connected.

"My duty to the Warlord, by eliminating you," Mandarr said, starting once more to reattach the phaser jumper.

Was Kyley so much of a machine now that the human remnant could survive in the thin atmosphere of Ehl? Or so casually contemplate Bhodi's death?

Feeling faint, Bhodi backed away, and almost allowed Mandarr to complete his task. He wondered why the Regulars had stopped firing, and cursed them for not taking the decision from him. There was a roaring in his ears so loud it was almost painful.

Then with sudden fury born of frustration, Bhodi began firing at everything on Mandarr's fighting suit that looked computerized, as though he meant to kill only that part of Mandarr and spare the rest. Snakelike conduits were sliced in half, some hissing invisible gases, others leaking steel-gray fluids. A black box on Mandarr's shoulder exploded in a shower of sparks.

Mandarr seemed almost not to notice. He calmly reconnected the umbilical, pointed his weapon at Bhodi's chest, and squeezed the trigger. Nothing happened—except in that moment, the roaring in Bhodi's ears resolved itself into individual voices on the omni circuit.

"Bhodi! Where's the Sarge? We've got two of the crystals back," a jubilant Pike was saying. "Another surprise. They had them cached out here, instead of holding them in the warren—"

"They're coming out!" Kree-tih was bellowing. "Four—six—seven Warri. I need support. Where's the support?"

Mandarr was intently twisting the damaged connector, trying to find a position where it would provide good contact. Bhodi saw a tiny blue light wink on above the pistol grip, blink out, then begin to shine steadily. He could not wait any longer. As Mandarr began to turn his weapon once more toward Bhodi, Bhodi raised the Allison and aimed it at Mandarr's unprotected head.

But even as his finger was curling against the contacts, Bhodi twitched the focus downward to Arrian's chest pod. His aim was true. He hit the pod squarely, and sinuous electric-blue sparks began to race up and down the length of Mandarr's body. There was a sizzling sound, like water on a hot griddle, and then a blinding white explosion that made Bhodi flinch and look away.

When he looked back, his friend and enemy was gone, without so much as a footprint left behind to show he had been there.

A shadow flashed overhead, and Bhodi looked up numbly to see the pod sweep in a tight half-circle and drop onto the crater floor. He took a few hesitant steps in that direction, then stopped to watch as Pike and two of the Regs dragged Li-hon's motionless body aboard. Almost without thinking, Bhodi scooped up the body of B'ere'a and carried it down to the pod.

"I have to go down after the crystal—" he said as a Reg came up to him and relieved him of his burden.

"Forget it," Pike barked from the hatchway, waving Bhodi in. "The clock's run out. Come on. This isn't going to be a very good place to be."

A minute later, the pod was screeching spaceward at maximum lift, while a poisonous black cloud boiled furiously upward and outward from the crater. All through the ascent, Bhodi stared down at the growing blemish on the face of the planet.

"I killed him," he said mournfully.

"No, you didn't," Parcival said, slipping into the seat beside him. "He was recalled to his ship. A hit on the chest pod breaks a trap-loop circuit and throws them back to their ship. For a while we were fighting the nasty myth that the Arrians aren't real—just projections, impossible to kill. Well, it's not impossible. But it's hard—as you saw.''

''But that was Evan Kyley—my friend—''

Parcival nodded. ''I know.''

''You knew?'' Bhodi demanded angrily, turning away from the window for the first time.

''The Sixth recruited him a year ago. He was captured in a fight on Deranis, and the Warlord made an experiment of him.'' Parcival shook his head. ''He's not the person you knew. He's controlled completely by his implants.''

''Why wasn't I told?''

''I don't know,'' Parcival said. ''I guess you think I should have told you.''

''Yeah, I guess I do.''

''Sorry, Bhodi. The Sarge gave us very clear orders. He didn't explain them.''

''The Sarge,'' Bhodi echoed, craning his head to look around the cabin. ''Where is he?''

''Down below, in an ice tank—''

Bhodi swallowed. ''Then he's—''

''Ice as in isolation, not as in 'on ice.' ''

A sigh of relief. ''How is he?''

''Not good, thanks to Mandarr. Not dead, thanks to you.'' Parcival glanced forward. ''There's *Zephyr* coming up. Almost home.''

''No,'' Bhodi said, looking back at the shadowed face of the planet. ''Nowhere near home.''

Li-hon was transferred directly from the pod's ice tank to one in *Zephyr's* tiny sick bay. He stayed there most of the way back to Intellistar, insensible to the world, healing his wounds with the remarkable regenerative power of the Qeth. The hole in his side closed over; new fingers grew where charred stubs had been; the crust covering the right half of his skull fell away to reveal new skin, pale green and unweathered.

When he opened his eyes at last, what he saw made him smile. Pike was perched on the edge of the adjoining bed, intently practicing card tricks which had economic rather than entertainment value.

"I guess I missed the last hand."

"Kind of," Pike said, looking up with a pleased expression on his face and letting the cards fall easily into one hand. "How are you feeling?"

"Tired. Hungry. I've been hurt worse. How did it fall out?"

"A mixed bag. We lost two—B'ere'a and Yiaj—"

"Was it Mandarr?"

"Yes."

"Did we get him?"

"No. Bhodi took him on—"

"Bhodi?"

"He was all right. Wait until you see the battle films from Kree-tih's camera. But the clock ran down before either of them could make a kill."

"Then we lost Ehl, too."

"Yes."

Li-hon frowned and shook his head. "The Arrians have always been tough, real tough. But up till now, they've never been *smart* fighters," he reflected. "If the other Arrian commanders start following Mandarr's example, we're going to be in for a hell of a time."

"Tomorrow's worry," Pike said. Then he added cheerfully, "We got two of the three crystals back."

"Did we! That's something," Li-hon said, settling back in the tank. "That and what I saw happen to Bhodi Li almost add up to a win."

Pike's expression darkened. "I should have said something sooner—"

"What?"

"It looks like Bhodi was a casualty, too. He's been in a shell since we left Cavalon, keeping to himself, not talking to anyone. It's different than the last time, though—not sulky. Something else, I don't know what."

"I think I do," Li-hon said slowly. "Let me sleep for a couple of hours. Then send him to me."

No one Christopher Jarvis had been close to had ever died, so he did not know if what he had been feeling since the fight on Ehl could be called mourning. Part of the problem was that he couldn't decide exactly which loss he was feeling more keenly—or even exactly when it had been lost.

He had lost Evan, that was for certain. There had been several points at which Bhodi had decided to stick it out precisely because he knew that he could have everything back simply by going home. But he no longer had that comfort. Evan was not backpacking across the country, too busy or too lazy to write. He was forever out of reach, fighting for the Warlord of Arr, made a traitor to his homeworld by a forest of wires buried in his brain.

But Bhodi had lost something else, too. Once and for all, he had learned that it was not a game. It had been a hard lesson, and long in coming. Even the skirmish at *Majestic* had not made the point—the one dead crew member he'd seen seemed like a prop, and the real violence had taken place off-stage, inside the ship and on top of the cliff. But when B'ere'a had screamed, and Li-hon went down, Bhodi had lost at last the lingering illusion that sometime the lights would come up and the players all go home.

Evan would not be going home. B'ere'a would not be going home. All comforts, all illusions, were gone—and perhaps that was what Bhodi was mourning.

It was on the heels of that insight that Pike came by with the message that Li-hon wanted to see him. Bhodi accepted the news with equanimity. He was not looking forward to hearing Li-hon's critique of his performance on Ehl, but there were things he needed to talk to the sergeant about.

He found Li-hon out of the ice tank and sitting on the edge of the surgical table. He was dressed in station fatigues, but bootless and beltless. Bhodi was amazed at how quickly his wounds had healed.

"Are you the same guy we put in here?" Bhodi asked. "I guess I don't have to ask you if you're going to be all right."

"Good genes," Li-hon said, smiling and tapping his chest. "How do you think I attract so many ladies?"

Bhodi smiled wryly. "You're probably wondering if *I'm* going to be all right," he said. "I guess Pike told you I've been hiding out."

"He did."

"Well—I had some things to think about." Bhodi paused, his head cocked to one side as he considered his next words.

"Such as—"

"If Mandarr could be captured—could he be helped?"

"It's possible," Li-hon said, not surprised by the question. "It's not likely. We don't have much experience with the kind of tampering he's been subjected to. And capturing him's not something you can take on yourself personally. We're fighting across a thousand-light-year front. The fact is that the Ninth may never come up against Mandarr again."

Bhodi flashed a quick, wistful smile. "I had to ask," he said. "Something else. Parcival said you gave orders for people not to talk to me about Mandarr—"

"Yes."

"Why?"

"You had too many selfish reasons for what you were doing. I didn't want to give you another one."

"That's fair," Bhodi said with a nod. "Was he part of the reason you recruited me?"

Li-hon crossed his arms over his chest. "In a coldly strategic sense, yes. I don't like the Warlord to have any asset that we can't balance. But I never planned to send you out to face him one-on-one as you were forced to do on Ehl. We fight as a platoon. There's no room for personal vendettas."

Bhodi seemed satisfied with that answer, too. "About going home—"

"I understand," Li-hon said with a barely audible sigh. "I'll see that your return is arranged, as I promised."

"You *don't* understand," Bhodi said. "I was wondering whether my training will pick up right away, or whether there'd be a chance to go back and take care of some things first. I'd like to get my family off that phantom timeline. And then I'd like to pick a better time and way to disappear, do a better job of saying goodbye. Because one of these times I might not come back."

"You want to continue?"

"If you'll have me."

"You know that I've always believed your promise was special," Li-hon said. "I saw nothing on Ehl to make me change my mind. The question has always concerned your commitment, not your heart or ability. So please forgive me for asking if you know what your reasons are for continuing your challenge."

"You want to know if this is because of Evan."

"Yes. I do."

"I can give you a quick answer, because I asked myself that question before I came down here," Bhodi said. "It's not about Evan."

"Good—"

"But it is about what the Warlord did to him. That showed me better than anything how little the Arrians care for what we are, and how casually they'd destroy it."

"What you say is true," Li-hon said. "And it's a hard truth for someone your age."

Bhodi shook his head. "I'm older than I look. See, I've spent these last two days putting away my childhood," he said. "Because this war is no place for children—and there's no place for me to be but here."

"Are you sure?"

"I'm sure."

Li-hon slipped down off the table. "We'll get you some time to go home," he said with a pleased smile. "But your training is over, Bhodi Li. You've learned what you most needed to. The rest you can learn as a Guardian."

A month had passed, most of it spent on Earth, before Li-hon's promise to Bhodi could be fulfilled. Then, in the company of the entire Ninth Platoon, he returned to the Sanctum for the first time since his encounter with the First Guardian following his audition on Rejia.

This time reminded him very much of the other. The stars still blazed through the nine great viewports, and the disk of the planet still appeared overhead in the octagonal skylight. The audience was the same—Parcival, Pike, Lord Baethan, Tivia, and Li-hon. Above the dais floated the image of the wise-faced, maternal First Guardian, garbed and coiffed just as before.

But as he stood in the middle of the circle and looked around him at the expressions on the others' faces, Bhodi realized that there was one immeasurable difference. This time, Bhodi knew he belonged.

"Welcome back, Bhodi Li," the First Guardian said. "Today you become one of the chosen, a Guardian of the

Light, a true Photon Warrior. Nar-lex-ko-li-hon, does he wear the ring?''

"He does, First Guardian," Li-hon said.

Bhodi glanced down proudly at the heavy metal jewelry decorating the third finger of his right hand. The ring bore not only the spectral disk of the Alliance, but the emblem of the Ninth Platoon as well.

"Nar-lex-ko-li-hon, as Bhodi Li's teacher and mentor, do you affirm his right and worth to wear the ring of a Guardian?"

"I do, First Guardian," Li-hon said.

"Bhodi Li, you have earned the right to a place among the Guardians of Light," said the First Guardian. "Twice you were asked to give up your challenge, and twice you refused. Now I ask you one final time to claim your place with us, or relinquish it forever. What is your choice?"

"I claim it," Bhodi said with a sideways glance at Li-hon, who was beaming like a proud father.

"Then give now your oath of allegiance—"

EPILOG

The throne room of Scarrcastle was a shadowy place at the heart of a forbidding world, an armed and cratered artificial world moving through the silent gloom of a dark nebula. A wraith, a changling, a horrible grotesquerie sat upon the throne of the Warlord of Arr and screamed its rage. A bizarre and hideous menagerie formed a loose circle around the throne, some standing, some crouching, some cringing.

"My Lord—" began one of the Warri.

The wraith's wail sharpened to a shriek.

"My liege," the Warri attempted bravely, "Mandarr has won a great victory for the Dark against the demon Nar-lex-ko-li-hon—"

"Nothing! The demon lives! The crystals lost!"

"But a world claimed for the Dark Alliance—"

"The new warrior," the Warlord roared. "He lives as well."

"Yes, my lord."

Smoke rose up from the throne and swirled around the Warlord. When it dissipated, he stood a foot taller, his features more horrible than ever. "I want him. I want him

214

mine. I want him dead.'' The words echoed the length of the long chamber.

The Warri bowed deeply. "Yes, my lord. But what threat is one thin-fleshed Guardian—"

"Do you question me?" the Warlord thundered.

"I question only—"

The wraith-changling shrank to a bristle-backed lump half its former height. "They will draw strength and courage from him. I sense it. I foretell it. Take your choice of my warriors. Find the new demon, and destroy him."

The Warri bowed again. "As you command. In the name of the Warlord, let the Darkness grow."

And the circle of monsters rose up as one to repeat in voices snarling, cold and terrible: "Let the Darkness grow!"

Worlds of action and adventure by
JERRY POURNELLE
Bestselling co-author of *Lucifer's Hammer*

Fantastic futures from
Ace Science Fiction

__	20671-9	The Endless Frontier	$3.50
__	22218-8	Exiles to Glory	$2.95
__	38291-6	Janissaries	$3.50
__	38298-3	Janissaries: Clan and Crown	$3.50
__	78583-2	A Step Farther Out	$3.50

PLUS— a riveting suspense series from Charter that Robert Heinlein called "The most realistic counterespionage story I've read in a long time."

__	71089-1	Red Heroin	$2.95
__	71092-1	Red Dragon	$2.95